Looking for
John Steinbeck

Other Books by Ginna Gordon:

The Honey Baby Darlin' Series
A serial memoir about cooking,
love, & the love of cooking

  Book One–The Farm

  The Gingerbread Farm

The Sunny Mae & Bird Read-Aloud Series
with illustrations by Dai Thomas

  Sunny Mae & Bird in Alaska

  Sunny Mae & Bird on Ice (Winter 2016)

First You Grow the Pumpkin:
100 Cool Things to Make and Preserve

The Marriage Tip Book:
Advice from the Wise Ones of the 2nd Grade
with Nan Heflin

A Simple Celebration:
The Nutritional Program from
the Chopra Center for Well Being
as Ginna Bell Bragg, with David Simon, MD
Foreword by Deepak Chopra (pub. by Random House)

Visit www.luckyvalleypress.com

Looking for John Steinbeck

Book One in *The Lavandula Series*
based on the fictional journals
of Stefani Michel

Ginna Gordon

Cover Art and Tiny Paintings by
Dai Thomas

Lucky Valley Press
2016

Looking for John Steinbeck

ISBN: 978-0-9967802-7-8

Book One in The Lavandula Series

Produced and Published in 2016 by Lucky Valley Press
Jacksonville, Oregon & Carmel, California
www.luckyvalleypress.com

Acknowledgements

My heartfelt thanks to the early readers of *Looking for John Steinbeck*, especially Dr. Frank "Doc" DeLuca, whose comment ("I didn't want it to end!") inspired me more than any applause ever. The other early readers, Gail Lindus & George Erwin, Christi Koelker, Ken Gregg, Dai Thomas, Randi Andrews, Patricia Vollmer, Joan Marsh, Katherine Edison, Nan Heflin and, of course, David Gordon, all count among my favorite people on earth and get gold stars for their honest comments and encouragement.

I thank the late and venerated John Steinbeck for being my writer's guru and inspiration, and Mr. Pat Hathaway of California Views Historical Photo Collection (online at www.caviews.com) for providing the John Steinbeck photo for my desk. Mr. Steinbeck looks right into my eyes every morning and says, "Do it."

I am grateful to Michael Hemp of the Cannery Row Foundation for curating the valuable history of the Row. Some folks have no idea that underneath the shops, restaurants, entertainment and amazing flora and fauna of Cannery Row and Carmel and all of the Monterey Peninsula, lie the bones of an awesomely interesting past. After enjoying the great cioppino or the pink cotton candy, visit Doc Ricketts' lab and hear the stories of that dusty apartment and the dank and mysterious lab downstairs. It is a gem of an experience.

Dai Thomas, another Carmel Valley local, continues to be my awesome art colleague, adding color and beauty to my written material. *The Lavandula Series* comes alive with her contributions, and her dedication to our art partnership is, in the word of my son, Michael Patterson, "epic."

I called Carmel Valley "home" for almost fifty years. Today, from my studio in Jacksonville, Oregon, I have perspective for writing about my adopted hometown, and my love affair with Carmel, its river, its valley, the bay, the illustrious history, its residents real and imagined, never ends. The list of characters in *The Lavandula Series*, in fact, includes the area itself, so ripe is it with fertile luster, so full of the Creator's awesome beauty.

And, speaking of the Creator, I give thanks for the power of creation, whatever positive and loving form it takes, clothes he or she wears. As Richard Farnsworth said in the movie *Resurrection*, "God is Love and Versa Visa."

Ginna Gordon

Jacksonville Oregon 2016

PS: As you read, you can consult the Bird's Eye View, Front Elevations, and Interiors which follow page 261 in this book.

For Bonne *"Babe"* Conroy

Dear Babe,

I dedicate the entire *Lavandula Series*
about sisters and cousins to you.

My biggest fan since the crib,
you are the sister I never had.

As a cousin, a young cohort,
and an old pal, you are the best.

Thanks for telling me to
stop everything else and write.

With love,

Your favorite cousin

GB

The Cast of Characters   *(Age in 1960)*

Jock "Poppy" Wyman, Patriarch	75
Maria "Mama Maria" Wyman, Matriarch	65

THEIR DAUGHTERS

Rita Grace Wyman Michel	35
Nancy "Nana" Wyman Huffington	32
Nora "Fox" Wyman	30

THE COUSINS

Stefani "Stevie" Awena Michel (Rita's daughter)	11
Jolene Huffington (Nana's daughter)	12
Tate Marie Wyman (Fox's daughter)	12

HUSBANDS/BFs

Stefáno "Fáno" Michel (Rita's husband, father of Stevie)	40
Charles "Chuck" Huffington (Nana's husband, father of Jolene)	38
Deke Harley (Fox's missing partner, father of Tate)	35

THE RODRIGUEZ FAMILY

Juana	38
Felix	40
Chico	3
Lady Charlotte Huffington (Charles's mother)	75

Author's Note

As the Wheel of Life turns at Sweet Farm, the homestead of the Wymans, a Carmel Valley, Calfornia family, we focus on three sisters: Rita, Nana and Fox, and their three daughters: Stevie, Tate and Jolene, cousins and friends.

Life rumbles the earth at the farm, like any compound full of women, their men, children, elders and friends. They breathe the air of the Valley, filled with the scent of lavender growing abundantly on ten fertile acres. They eat of the garden harvest. The women are restless. The men are nervous. The girls are growing up in the 60s and they and their peers will become known as Baby Boomers, Flower Children, Hippies, Yuppies, the ME generation; they will be affected by the Vietnam War, Rock & Roll, revolutions from sexual to political, and dramatic social change. But, mostly, they will be dealing with their loves, children and homes as they relate to and are touched by those issues described above.

Looking for John Steinbeck, Book One in *The Lavandula Series*, sets the scene for the saga of the Wymans, their offspring and relations, with Charles Huffington, Jolene's father, as he contemplates his recent behavior.

Prologue

Can a man think out his life, or must he just tag along?

– John Steinbeck

November 1960

Sweet Farm, Carmel Valley, California
Chuck at the Rock – Schulte Road Bridge

Charles Huffington huddled on his rock under the Schulte Road Bridge, quaking like one of the nearby river-hugging willows in the chilled and impatient November air. The wind whipped Chuck's shaggy blonde hair into his face. It picked up the tail of his wrinkled blue Brooks Brothers shirt and flapped it against his cold backside. His jacketless body was just one of his issues. His shivers, and the hairs standing on end, on his arms and under his socks and on his temples and slowly creeping into the sensitive hollows behind his ears, came from other and more compelling sources than lack of layers: fear, loneliness, despair, shame, DTs.

The Carmel Valley night sky was clear, full of stars, the moon bright and close to fullness. The stark sky was crystalline, calling, begging Charles to look upward to share its sparkling pulchritude, but Charles's eyes were clouded with tears.

1

In a shaky hand, he addressed an envelope to his mother by flashlight, unaware of the call of the stars above him, the soft breeze on the path rustling the willows, the trickling, tinkling sound of the river splashing its way over rocks that usually made him want to unzip his trousers and water a bush. He stopped to light a cigarette, curving his body and cupping his hand over the Zippo. He brushed sparking ashes off his bare arm, exposed by rolled-up shirt cuffs. His trembling fingers slipped and poked the ballpoint pen through the paper several times, staining his khaki pants.

Lady Charlotte Huffington

Buchram Place

London SE

Christ Almighty, Chuck mumbled to himself as he scratched his note. He sniffled his running nose and wiped the tears he wasn't crying onto his sleeve. *How could I have done that? I don't even like Fox Wyman. Hghmph. I don't really like her perfect sister, Nana either, but look at that mess! 14 years of that! Ugh! What am I doing? Well, I know what to do now. I've been working up to this. It's settled then.*

Chuck finished his writing business, sluiced icy-cold Carmel River water over his not-crying face to clear the not-cried tears and trudged his way back up Schulte Road to the farm. He took his time. No country boy, our Charles Huffington: his nocturnal peregrinations were few, and his shoes were slip-on, thin-soled, citified. He waved his little flashlight into the bushes, spotted the bright orange eyes of a fox, or maybe that was a raccoon. No more foxes for him! He scratched his way along the pavement for about three hundred yards until, in his beam of battery-operated luminosity, he picked up Sweet Farm's dirt driveway to the left.

He stopped by the blue VW Split Window Sedan, new to him and Nana, but old to someone: rust peeled the paint off by layers—brown-sugary crusts attesting to years of Pacific Ocean-side parking. He placed the addressed and stamped envelope on top of his suitcase in the tiny backseat. He retrieved his jacket from the front seat and put it on. His feet whispered up the walkway to the house. He carefully slid open the glass door, stepped in, closed the door behind him, took off his shoes, gathered them under his arm, and in his stocking feet, crept into the Adobe House, his home for almost twelve weeks, like a cat burglar. He slowly sock-skated to the piano, picked up some papers off the bench and tiptoed down the hall into Jolene's room. He tapped her on the shoulder and Jolene jumped awake with a yelp.

"Sssshhhhh... It's OK, Joey, it's me. Daddy."

"What is it? You all right?" Her voice was sleepy, surprised.

"Spiffing, Poppet. Come out to the yard so we have pr-r-r-i-ivacy." Pr-r-i-i-vacy. Was he slurring his words? His Britishness got all uppity when he was drinking, compensating. Even Jolene at 12 got that. In his right hand he held some papers close to his chest and over that, in his left hand, his conductor's baton.

Jolene looked at her clock. "Daddy, It's 2 in the morning. Can't this wait?"

"No. No..." he whispered as he slipped on his shoes. He was clearer-eyed by then, the splash of water and late night walk home in the wind having braced his shakes a little, but the distress surely showed on his face. "No, it definitely cannot wait. I have a train to catch. I have to go. I have to go."

"OK, Chuck," sighed the nervous Jolene. *Crapola.* She didn't like this at all. *What's a girl supposed to do here?* "I'll get Nana." Her mother might know what to do.

"No! Oh, God, no, you can't. No, don't do that. This is the point. No Nana. Come with me. Outside. Please."

"Right. OK. OK." Jolene grabbed her robe and slippers. Whatever this was, good or bad, she was now in the middle of it. She sighed. *In the Middle Again. A good song title for Tate.* She followed her father out the bedroom door and right out the little side door into the yard, away from the windows.

When he judged they were far enough away from the house to speak, Chuck faced his daughter, took her by the shoulders to steady his hands and whispered, deliberately, "Joey, I am leaving. I am going on a trip. I am going for a job. But, don't tell, Jo. Don't tell anyone. You've got to give me time to get away, because they'll want to stop me, so don't tell. I want you and *only you* to know this."

"But, where are you going, Daddy? I thought you had a job here, at Sweet Farm? Why are you leaving? Are you coming back?"

"I will be back, Poppet. I am going to get that conductor job, but ssshh... They don't think I have it in me, but they're wrong. They're wrong. I can't stay here. I can't pick the bloody lavender. I can't look at my hands anymore, or do any of this. But you, you have to keep my secret. Keep my secret, honey, OK? Do not tell them."

"Daddy, have you been drinking? Are you planning on driving?"

"I'm fine. I'm fine. Sober as a judge. Clear as a bell. Solid as a rock. For the first time in eons. Honestly. I just needed to tell you I'm going. And I'll be calling you in three days time from my hotel room in New York, so you'll be the first to know the good news."

"It's not good news that you're leaving, Daddy."

"Yes, yes, it is. I'll get this job and I'll send for you."

"No, you won't. But if you need this, OK, I won't tell."

In silence and wonderment at her beauty and perfection, Chuck looked at his daughter. His only ally. Oh, wait. His responsibility! *But, no. Really. She's better off this way. I must do this.* He made her promise she would not tell.

"There's nothing for me here, Poppet, but you." *And now you have to watch me go. I'm sorry.*

And with that, Chuck pulled himself up to his full height, pushed all thoughts of who and what he was leaving out of his carefully corralled mind and boldly stepped into his future self, like slipping inside a new body, a whole different person.

He flung his errant thoughts away, a burdensome old coat, and focused on the path. One. Foot. In. Front. Of. The. Other.

He kissed his daughter on the nose, walked steadily to the old battered Bug and, in order to keep its rasping, choking, coughing, sputtering lurch into action from waking the entire Sweet Farm compound full of Nosy Parkers nestled snug and oblivious in their dozen or so beds, he pushed it down the dirt driveway to Schulte Road. He kept pushing until his sound effects were buffered by an old stand of bushy cypress trees. Then he jumped in and, with the usual rumble and cough under the hood, started up the car and was gone.

Jolene stood goose-bumped in the dark. She felt the weight of this secret knowledge like the burden of chain mail on her chest. She listened to the VW rumble away west on Carmel Valley Road and imagined her father at the wheel, whizzing by Felipe's Fruit Stand, changing into his white tie and tails while driving at 80 miles an hour, slicking back his hair with Brylcreem (a little dab'll do ya!), whipping out his baton which sparked and smoked and cooked itself right into a magic wand, while he transformed himself into *Super Conductor*, his alter-ego, his joke on himself, his best Self, he said, when looking at photos or in the mirror, ready to walk onto a stage or conductor's podium. He was just looking for that Self. She knew he'd lost it. They didn't joke about it any more.

She thought about getting her mother up—but then, what would Nana do now? Chase after him? No way. She wouldn't. She hardly noticed his existence these days.

No, Jolene promised her dad. *Maybe this is really what he needs. His dragon to slay. The start of a new day. I have to give him this.*

She thought he was dry. Or at least not drunk. *I didn't ask him what he was going to do about the car. Maybe I'm dreaming.*

Jolene went back to bed, but did not sleep until dawn, thinking about the Super Conductor and his magic wand.

Chapter One
Pack a Bag, Poppet

I have more memories than if I were a thousand years old.
— Charles Baudelaire

The universe is made of stories, not atoms.
— Muriel Rukeyser

Three months earlier – August 1960

High in the sky with the Huffingtons

Jolene was queasy and green. She could see the cigarette smoke moving through the cabin of the plane, billows of clouds rippling, intersecting, blending, drifting away. Jolene really wanted to get up and move about, perhaps throw up, but her father, Chuck, sprawled in the aisle seat, his right arm flung over her lap, those long legs spread out, one under the seat in front of Jolene, one twitching in the aisle, a ready obstacle to an unsuspecting stewardess in straight blue skirt, stockings and high heels. He slept.

Good, I guess, Jolene thought. *I haven't seen him sleep much lately. Too busy being a complete cabbage head.*

Jolene Huffington sat squashed between her silent parents in an airplane packed with summer travelers, *Yuck!* A big man in a button-bursting Hawaiian shirt and khaki shorts made tugboat rumbles in his sleep, furr-r-r-rling his lips and letting loose undignified slurpy sounds on exhale; a mother nursed her cranky baby, whose tiny fists punched the air—bam, bam; two children sniffled and squirmed, apathetically fighting over a comic book; a suntanned woman with bangles and red lipstick read a thick romance novel. Jolene saw the cover: bare-from-the-waist-up well-muscled hunk hugging perfect long-haired, wind-whipped beauty with torn bodice. White Shoulders perfume hung in the rarefied air around this bronzed & bangled romance reader, mixing with the cigarette smoke. *Gag.*

Jolene's mother, Nana, stared out the little window into the blue sky and somewhere beyond. Every now and then, Jolene saw her mother's jaw flex and quiver when she gritted her teeth. Nana's fingers drummed on the tray table in front of her, tapping a staccato tattoo with her shiny neutral-polished nails.

I can't walk down that aisle again, anyway, Jolene thought. *At least a hundred people observed my little personal crisis. No, I'll have to sit here and tough it out. Maybe I can reach the air vent thingy up there. Crikey, I need air. How many hours to go?* She looked at her watch. *Three more hours of this plane. Then what? San Francisco and... Sweet Farm! Hours to go! Sweet Farm is, like, light years away from San Francisco.*

I wonder, what's going to happen to my stuff in London?

August 1960

In the Hobbit House
Sweet Farm, Carmel Valley, California
Waiting for Jolene

 Stevie

My father, Fáno Michel, was always promising things. He'd flash that pearly-toothed, dimpled smile at me and say: "Stevie, ma chérie, of course I'll do eet. Ze next time your mother lets go of my apron str-r-rings."

Or he'd wipe his brow in mock over-worked exhaustion, and whisper, "Stevie, my zweet petunia (peh-too-nee-ya!), please let me feeneesh theez one task so mebbe I can do theez thing for you."

Or even on his knees, arms lifted to the sky: "Wena, my muse, my girl, any moment your gracious grandfather weel have nothing for me to do. Then? Voi! la!"

There is always tomorrow: Fáno's version of mañana. But, I knew he would come through. Sooner or later.

Still, Tate and I were scrunched in the too small Hobbit House, our private club in an oak tree. We waited now for the third cousin, Jolene, whom we hadn't seen in donkeys' years, on her way from the San Francisco airport. We had no illusions about Fáno's personal schedule. He'd either be along today or tomorrow. Probably next week. Mebbe.

Misty, our little beagle, pressed close to the trunk of the tree in her favorite shady spot, legs twitching, chasing dream cats, catching, letting go, chasing again. Tate ran her fingers under her bare thigh, groped for what was poking her, found the twig and tossed it out the door, where it dropped to the ground, three feet below. Misty opened one eye, blinked and snuffled back to sleep, to chase again.

Tate's loose fine hair swung around and grazed my teeth, blurring the words out of my mouth.

"Mrfft."

It was August, 1960, and it was hot.

In the relative cool of the Hobbit House, I sat cross-legged at the little table, scribbling notes about the forces of nature that were my parents, Rita and Fáno. That morning, in the Sweet Tea Room, Fáno hummed and whistled with a twinkle in his eye and Rita, my mother, dressed in a white T-shirt and black pants, made bread and soup and whatnot, unaware of the hand-shaped flour print on her behind.

I was deep in thought about Rita and Fáno, what I could say that wasn't trite, since they appalled and fascinated me at once,

12

when Tate, home from her Saturday piano lesson, appeared in the Hobbit House door. She climbed in, stirred up a puff of dust, and settled beside me. Her head touched the ceiling.

Looking out the window, Tate said, "Tch! I can't see down the driveway from in here. It's just too danged small and the tree's gotten too big and bushy! Ugh! I feel like Alice down the rabbit hole after she polished off that 'Eat Me!' cake."

Tate's bony elbow whacked me in the jaw.

"Ow-w-w!"

"Sorry. We need more room, Stevie. Face it. We are grown up now."

"Speak for yourself. Could you move your *butt* about five inches?" I stacked my yellow pad and a sheaf of drawings on top of my book, put my pens and pencils back in the little wooden box and slid it all under the table.

My grandfather, Jock Wyman, also known as Pop or Poppy, provided my first journal that summer before my 12th birthday, calling me a "precocious little troublemaker" with too many words in my mouth for someone my age. But he said it with a smile on his face, like he was secretly proud of his young protégé but wouldn't admit it in a million years, just to keep me on my toes.

The journal became such a part of my life that, as an ongoing Honors English project, the Sweet Farm memoir would occupy me for many years. Certain Dominican nuns have more tolerance of the bare truth than others and I was fortunate that my Guidance Counselor slash Home Room slash English &

Drama teacher, Sister William, had an open mind. Otherwise, I hated school and was bored by it. But, she saw to it that I was always motivated, kept me writing and observing, even when I was turned off and dulled to tarnished silver by Sisters Delmonico and Jordon, who called me Steffie, and treated me like an urchin with dirt under my nails and snot in my nose and beneath their dignity. Sister William had a plan to see my head opened up and packed with whatever knowledge she had at her fingertips.

The journal, a thick artist's pad in a leather sleeve, came wrapped in gold foil with a big red bow. Jock, Poppy, also mentioned that to be a good writer, one had to be a good listener. "So, stop talking and listen to everything," he said. "Ideas come from everywhere." And he knew. We lived in Steinbeck Country because Jock Wyman was a good listener.

Five years in England!" Tate said. She had Brit-envy in her eyes. We weren't in touch with Jolene over the last five years, but we were surely bumpkins compared to her.

"Travels abroad!"

"Goes to school in London!"

"Fashion-plate!"

"Hats for the High Church of England!"

"British accent!"

We were country girls: organized by Dominican sisters at Santa Lucia School in Monterey from September to June; in our tree all summer; and convinced, as only girls verging on their individual hormonal crises can be, that everyone else in the entire universe was more interesting/beautiful/talented/smart/lucky/you-name-it than we were, especially Jolene—well, I thought so, anyway—everything in her life must be so... cool. So... sophisticated. She must have the world on a string!

In madras short-shorts and men's white t-shirts (lifted from Fáno's closet), sleeves rolled a la James Dean (sans the pack of cigs), arms and legs tan from long sunny days on Sweet Farm, we sat huddled together. Tate's hair: long, fine, blonde and swinging, a few leaves and twigs caught in it like bugs in a web. Mine: dark and dense, hanging down my back in a thick and messy braid.

Grown up. Ha... ha... ha. Precocious troublemakers.

The journal from Poppy was the beginning of my life's work: words became my passion, my observations fodder and my imagination fuel for stories. No incident or activity was safe from my gaze.

James Dean died on my seventh birthday. I wasn't really into him at seven, but, later, at the advanced age of ten, I warmed to his style. We made similar clothing choices: jeans, denim jacket. I added the white T-shirt to the ensemble after seeing one of his moody photos with a cigarette dangling out of his beautiful pouty mouth. Oh, it was great that we had so much in common (sans the cigs, again).

"What did your mom tell you last night?" Tate whispered in my ear. I don't know why, no one was listening, but we stage-whispered in the Hobbit House. "Why are they suddenly coming to Carmel Valley?"

"Dunno, really. Aunt Nana sounded peevish."

"You talked to her?"

"No, but I could hear the tone of her voice, like she was in a tunnel, far away in England, on a pay phone, maybe, and... PO'd."

Kids can tell if there is peevishness in the air, can't they? Like cats: ears twitch at the slightest change in vibe.

"Where are they going to live? Please tell me, no one will be crammed with us in the Barn. I like her: Jolene, I mean. Well, I did five years ago, but, I was eight! And my Cube is so small. And Chuck!"

I knew what she meant. Tate had a lot of stuff in small quarters. And, Uncle Charles... well, he was... we'll get along to Chuck here, soon enough.

"With Mama Maria and Poppy. They tidied up the spare bedroom, your mom & Aunt Nana's old room, I mean, and while you've been gone today they took all the office file boxes out of the storage room, Rita's old room, and they're going to have it painted. Your little Cube is safe. Rita says they're crashing your mom's party, but I didn't know Aunt Fox was giving one."

"She's not, silly. I think that means they will be spoiling my mother's carefully organized little play called, 'Pretend You're the Son They Always Wanted.' Or worse, 'Pretend You're Deke.' She's been running this place for ten years now. You'd think she'd be comfortable with it. But, she doesn't want either one of those Huffingtons meddling in her Sweet Farm. She'd hate to lose control."

"But they've been here before!"

"Yeah, but only to visit—not to stay. And not with Jolene since we were practically babies!"

"Yeah. Fourth of July of '55."

"And besides, can you imagine Chuck or Nana running Sweet Farm?" She laughed.

But I had already left for the beach in my head. Fourth of July '55. The fog was socked in like a wet, dripping blanket over all of Carmel, but we stayed in the sand and surf all day: Tate, Jolene and I built sand castles...

 Tate

Approaching 13, I was all arms and legs, angles and sharp edges, tall and pointy, but Stevie was round and sweet, soft and dark, and no matter how much she overtly resisted her secret exotic heritage, it draped over her like a cape of peacock feathers. She was amazing. All that prattle about feeling inferior, was mostly me.

All I needed was another smart, gorgeous cousin on the compound. Or some bossy-pants. I'd hate that. At least Stevie was young enough, and, uhm, small enough, to lean on me a bit. It was a total sham, you know, that because I was older, I was wiser. She was light-years ahead of me. And daring.

Stevie had these big ideas about *Jolene*. It was *Jolene* this and *Jolene* that, and when *Jolene* gets here, we'll... whatever.

But I... I didn't know. I was doubtful. Jolene could be big trouble. Her parents were giant emotional trouble-making machines.

Or worse... she was perfect.

My mind was clear on these things:

I was an ugly duckling;

I was tone deaf and off pitch;

I was a danged *bastard*, that's enough right there;

not to mention tall,

skinny,

flat

and invisible.

Pack a Bag, Poppet

 # Jolene

So, which was worse: my parents' knock down-drag out, full-on, red-letter, hot-ticket fights? Or the long, frost-bitten silences that seeped like ice into my 12-year-old heart, froze it and then broke it apart, with a sledge hammer, leaving little icebergs in my blood.

Well. I'd say the silences win that one.

At least with a full-on fight you have inflammatory words and confessed secrets to ponder. Am I being over-dramatic?

But just at the moment in question, the car was hot – the air, thick as jam. I hung my head half out the window. Poppy drove down Carmel Valley Road like he was trotting some old nag ponies along in a buggy, so there wasn't exactly a cool breeze. But I was glad to be out of planes.

Nana hunched into the other corner of the backseat. I avoided her gaze, since silence was the day's script—a page full of zed. When my mum had her ire up, you could see the steam coming from her ears. It practically sizzled in the hot air. I suppose words weren't really necessary, since her body language was so expressive.

Nana and Chuck, my father, hadn't spoken—not even a hghmph!—in eight hours, since the last argument regarding hauling the luggage down the stairs from our hotel room in New York because they didn't have the cash to tip the porter.

I came home to the London flat one morning earlier that week from a sleepover and found my father in a sort of heap on the floor, his face chalk white, with my mother sitting in a chair holding a splintered hunk of wood in one hand and a glass of red wine in the other. They were strained, edgy, like they had been up all night, which I found later to be true. I also discovered, much later, of course, that my mum had not whacked my father upside the head, which had been my first thought. That is what it looked like. That morning glass of wine was odd, too. Well, it was bad. It was all bad. I did notice the door looked a bit knocked up, but it took days to piece the puzzle together. In the meantime, I was told we were "going to California, Poppet. Pack a bag."

One thing I learned, living with Nana and Chuck: explanations for their actions were not always immediately handy. I took a deep breath and went to my room to pack, hoping for a clue-in. I had no idea "going to California" actually meant "escaping to California."

In the car, riding shotgun, Chuck barely answered Poppy's jolly questions, which I thought were forced on Poppy's part. He was trying too hard. Chuck answered "Yes" and "No" and "I don't know yet." Flat.

Nana mouthed silent invectives toward the reflection in the window. I couldn't tell what. It didn't matter. She'd been doing it all day. She'd been doing it for years.

I entertained myself by calculating Stevie's and Tate's ages and what they would be like now. Will they still like me? We had a jolly good time together, but, that was before. Before all this.

I lay my head back on the seat and remembered the walks down the road to the bridge—what was it? Shultz? Schulte Road! Beyond the lavender fields, down the little hill, across the one lane bridge and then around and down into the riverbed, whispering, "lions and tigers and bears, oh my!" And something about Mack and... and frogs.

And the 4th of July picnic on the beach, sheltered in a cove of those big streaky boulders. Aunt Rita gave me a brown, nubbly cable knit sweater she'd made for Uncle Fáno, which hung down over my body like a woolly dress. Fáno brought three loads of firewood down to the beach and kept the fire going all day and into the misty evening. We built sand castles with Aunt Fox and played in the surf and popped bulbs of kelp with our feet in the sand. We roasted hot dogs and marshmallows. Aunt Rita gave us cups of hot tea with honey. The sparklers fizzled in the fog. Funny, I don't remember my father in this picture at all, though I know he was there.

I loved the wet, gritty sand on the bottoms of my feet when we walked up the granite steps from the beach to Scenic Drive. I rinsed them off in the little spigot of freezing cold water and Stevie handed me a small white terry towel out of her satchel. Mica-flecked sand was sprinkled in her dark eyebrows and in a swath across her chest. In her green shimmery bathing suit, with a big towel wrapped around her middle and dragging on the ground behind, and that long, dark, thick, wet hair streaming down her back, she was a mermaid, slithering across the walkway. She turned and smiled at me.

Oh, crikey and blast it, I thought, sitting in the backseat of Poppy's car. *Nana and Chuck have ruined everything, once again. Nothing good can come of this. I just know it. It's like they own the whole story, they're the puppeteers of a little marionette opera, and I'm just an extra, a wooden doll, pulled along by the strings attached to my shoulders and elbows. Dangling along. Fa la la.*

In the beginning there was nothing, which exploded.

–Terry Pratchett

EARLIER THAT MORNING

New York

Nana counts to ten

Earlier that morning, Nana Huffington stood in the dimly lit, dingy little airport hotel room, jet-lagged but elegant in khaki and white linen, gold charm bracelet dangling, ready to go. She stood by the open suitcases spread out on the rumpled twin beds. She looked at the wall with tired eyes, breathing very slowly, counting flowers in the faded wallpaper in order to get to ten, before she exploded. 6... 7... 8... 9...

She turned to look at Charles, who had slumped, sighing, weary and indifferent, into the chair by the hotel room's one window.

"Charles. Please, Charles. Stop moping about."

"I'm not moping, Nana. I am thinking." Charles had a wounded expression: Hang Dog, Rita would say. Squashed Bug, Nana said. He turned the old, faded chintz chair toward the window and gazed out on the Idlewild Airport maze.

Jolene lay on her little folding cot and watched the two of them go around and around. *Who would win? Neither,* she thought. *They are doomed down the drain, and I am going down with them. Glug, glug, glug...*

"Well stop thinking then. It's getting on my nerves. Think quietly, anyway. Quit fidgeting."

"Why are *your* knickers in a twist, Nana? It's *I* who have lost face... It's *my* reputation."

"Yes, Chucky Boy, actually, it is true. This one's all yours. So, just own up to this mess and get on. The money's gone, the deals are over, we've been chucked out, for heaven's sake! We are going home, my home, with our tails between our legs. That is why my precious knickers are in a twist. Everything is gone, Chuck."

"I've apologized over and over, Nana. What more do you want?"

Nana scowled. "I am so over apologies, Charles. It's too late. Your money is gone, our savings depleted, Jolene's college fund... amazingly, ohhh, what? Disappeared! And to top it all off, I've quit a very promising job to give us time out of England at Sweet Farm to figure out a way to deal with *your* bloody debt and save *your* bloody face from all the embarrassing muck you've stirred up with your dramas. You're sotted with gin. You've left a great wake behind you, with no easy solutions. The whole thing is a mess of colossal proportions. No. No apologies. No trust. No."

My college fund? Jolene blinked back a rush of tears. *This is the first I've heard of this.*

"You'll hold it over my head for years," Chuck said.

"It's not just the money. It's our lives, Chuck." Nana pronounced this last like she was spitting out a nail. "It's everything."

AUGUST 1960
Sweet Farm
Arrival

 Stevie

We were easily amused, Tate and I, and filled our time during the wait for Jolene and her parents with abundant family palaver. We worked out comfortable positions on the cushions, leaned back against opposite walls. It was the coolest spot on the compound on a warm summer afternoon. If a bit squashed.

The Hobbit House nestled like Horton the Elephant in a runtish but worthy oak tree between the Chapel House, my home on the compound, which I will describe shortly, and the Adobe House, where my grandparents lived, at the west side of Sweet Farm. The Hobbit House belonged solely to the cousins: Tate and me. And now, Jolene.

We were beside ourselves with excitement to share all this with her—the Hobbit House and our Girl Cousins' Club. No Boys Allowed, No Parents, except in emergencies, which totalled none thus far.

The three redwood slats nailed into the oak tree trunk formed a rickety ladder. The Hobbit House perched on a low branch, with a redwood platform, three feet up, four feet squarish.

Scraps of this and that, wood, branches, old fence posts, made wobbly walls, and we sat comfortably on the floor without bumping our heads, until that summer, when Tate grew three inches overnight. Three funky 12-inch windows were chiseled out, no glass, with yellow checked cotton curtains thumb-tacked up in soft pleats on the inside. Our grandmother, Mama Maria, contributed a piece of beige shag carpet. With my mother's kitchen scissors we cut the door cover out of a canvas tarp: a raggedy roll-down shade over the opening facing east to the morning sun.

The roof, a combination of twigs and moss and slats all a-jumble and filled with an assortment of glittery baubles, contributed to the fantasy of our elvish selves, with pointy ears and delicate wings, living in a tree. Although we eschewed the hairy flat feet of Hobbits, the name stuck to our house, and we were satisfied.

Tate and I sprawled on our pillows and munched cherries, gossiping: complete hearsay, of course, especially anything to do with Uncle Charles. We had no idea what Chuck had been doing for the past five years, just wild guesses from overheard *sotto voce* conversational fragments in the night. The folks didn't discuss Chuck out loud. And Aunt Nana was always fun to dissect.

Had Aunt Nana bleached or dyed her hair, like she said she would when the early-onset grey took over? What color would it be? I wondered if Jolene's hair lightened, like her mother promised, or was it still Hibiscus red? Was she pretty? Still a tomboy? Would she fit into the Hobbit House? Fit with us? Would we like her? Would she like us? Is it D.I.V.O.R.C.E.?

"Girls?" My mother called to us.

"Up here, Rita. In the Hobbit!" I peeked through window to see her outline in the shadows.

Rita was shaped like Marilyn Monroe, only 4'10"—everything about my mother was in miniature. Her hair flounced around her face like corn silk with a curly attitude—hair I did not get. I took after my father, through and through, not one thing like my mother's people. If I ever ran off to my father's caravan family, like I fantasized regularly, I'd have fit right in.

Only there was no family. That August, 1960, I was still trying to convince Fáno to tell me the tale, but so far, he said no.

"No, my leetle zugar lump. Eet eez not a story I weesh to tell right now. Some day, mebbe. Not now."

"Come down now and clean up," Rita said. "Poppy just rang from the pay phone at the market—they'll be here in fifteen minutes."

It was Saturday evening. Rita and Fáno had been in the garden all afternoon.

Here's the funny thing: in the kitchen, Rita and Fáno were goofy and playful, always joking, sparks flying. In the garden, they worked alongside each other in complete silence, communicating in some kind of subtle non-verbal, private language: wind whispers, Rita-Fáno-ese. Whole sentences, complete thoughts were passed between them without a sound: with the flick of an eye, the brush of a hand, a wink, a sigh. They pulled weeds and raked and planted and watered, all in a kind of dance, to a tune no one could hear, in a place no one could visit.

Even though they were so happy with each other and themselves that they often forgot I was there (which could be lonely, even in the midst of a big family) even so, I was lucky. My parents never quarreled, like Aunt Nana and Uncle Chuck. And Fáno hardly left Rita's side: he wouldn't have thought of taking off, like Deke Harley, the Mystery Man, Tate's missing father.

At 13, Tate didn't remember much about Deke, except the whiff of English Leather always made her cry. I was just a baby when Deke disappeared. He never showed to meet Aunt Fox and Tate on a Saturday afternoon at the Salinas Rodeo in 1950. Fox waited about an hour, pushing Tate's stroller back and forth, back and forth. She started to worry. Then, she got ferociously mad. Then, she cried. Finally, she called Poppy from the Rodeo Grandstand office while the heat-bedraggled receptionist walked the floor with the restless, sweating 2½ year old. Half an hour later, Poppy picked them up in Salinas and brought them home. Mama Maria gave them cool things to drink and Fáno & Rita soothed their brows. And they waited, figuring Deke was carousing somewhere with rodeo buddies and would show up when he could drive. He'd done it before.

That Salinas Rodeo was ten years ago, and still no Deke Harley.

We wiggled our way out of the Hobbit and ran up to the Adobe House.

I didn't feel grown up—flat as a Monopoly board. And Tate had these little headlights on her chest, on permanent high beam, just like her mom.

 Jolene

My parents made it hard to like them. Perpetual frowns. Harsh words. Or no words at all for lo-o-ng stretches of time. Dissent. Histrionics galore.

Love them? Absolutely.

Like them? Right then? Not much.

I wonder if they could ever have worked it out. As it happened, they didn't have time, but we didn't know that then.

Nana and Charles's life together was a big fiasco, occasionally interrupted by hot frenetic physicality, usually in some inappropriate place. They didn't know I was on to them. Sometimes they were buffered by alcohol in the early evening, especially Chuck, anesthetized into peaceful coexistence, which lasted about an hour until one of them would hit the red button. Usually Nana.

"Where were you last night?"

"With Steven, working out the plan."

"Oh, yeah. Right then. And which plan is that? The Onboard Cruising Orchestra? £3,000 down the drain. Or was it the Airport Reunion Cafe? Had something to do with that blonde girl, Melayna Whatsit. About £15,000, as I remember..."

"Nana..."

"Or it must be the new Lo-o-ndon Lo-o-unge..." She stretched that one out like a long silky sound-ribbon.

On the way to Sweet Farm from the airport, our stop at the market allowed Chuck to schlump in to buy several hide-able bottles of gin in paper sleeves and a carton of Benson & Hedges to fill in the gaps between snorts, Nana to purchase the unmentionables, which I was too embarrassed to mention, and Poppy filled Maria's and Aunt Rita's lists.

I got American coins from Poppy and paid 10¢ for a frosty Coke in a bottle, 5¢ for a Hershey Bar, and 25¢ for a tiny tin of 6 aspirin, and slunk outside to wait.

I was nervous.

My family was a hopeless mess. Woolsley School, Fortnum & Mason, lovely afternoon teas with jam and toast and egg... Piccadilly... far, far away.

I could make babies, but had not reached the age of consent! I couldn't even date. Crikey, I had to borrow the first unmentionables from the stewardess.

My boobs were big bobbing balloons.

My hair was still finger-in-the-electric-socket-frizzy.

And red.

Red. Red. Red.

 Tate

We washed and brushed and dried faster than usual, put on sandals and raced out to the circular driveway where we gathered to welcome the Huffingtons, just arriving from London, by way of New York and San Francisco. There were nine of us, ten with Poppy: Mama Maria, Aunt Rita, Uncle Fáno, my mother, called Fox (because of the orangey color of her hair and eyelashes and the penetrating yellow-gold of her eyes—even her nose was fox-ish, long and thin and into your business), Stevie, me and the three Rodriguezes.

There were so many mothers at Sweet Farm—my mom, Aunt Rita, Maria, Juana, and the soon to arrive Nana—when someone yelled, "Mother!" or "Mom!" or "Mama!" they all looked up. First names delivered better results.

I had songs running in my head, something maybe I could sing later to say *Hello, Welcome Home.* I wanted to be nice. I couldn't decide if it was *Welcome Home*, or *Welcome to My World*, or *I am Sorry*, or *Does it Make You Cry When You Want to Laugh*? This last was just a title I'd made up for a country song, but promising lyrics floated in my brain.

Stevie and I belted out *The Indian Love Call.* "When I'm calling yo-o-o-o-o-o-o-u." And then, *Onward Christian Soldiers.* We marched around the circle a few times and then sang at the tops of our voices—*She wore an itsy-bitsy-teeny-weeny yellow polka dot bikini*, wiggling our boyish hips.

Soon we were gesturing wildly on air trombones: boom, boom, boom, boom, *76 Trombones led the big parade...* I was doing my best imitation of Harold Hill, the ersatz Music Man, leading the boys astray. Then we saw them.

Poppy was driving the brand-spanking-new 1960 black-and-shiny-as-patent-leather Cadillac Fleetwood, silver-tipped fins glinting in the sunlight, slowing down on Carmel Valley Road preparing to turn right on Schulte Road and right into our driveway.

Stevie bumped into my back as we abruptly halted in the midst of: *And we've got trouble! Right here!* Oomph!

We could see the shadow of Aunt Nana in the back seat and some hibiscus-red cotton candy fluttering out the opposite window. Uncle Chuck was scrunched down in the front, riding shotgun. Poppy concentrated on turning just so, to avoid scraping the new car on the Sweet Farm rock.

 Stevie

Poppy exploded like a fire cracker out of the driver's side of his spiffy new car, wearing blue jeans with rainbow suspenders and a green plaid shirt with the cuffs rolled up, over a long-sleeved red t-shirt, and his "What the hell is up with these people?" frown-wrinkled brow-smirk combo. He put his black and red "Please Feed the Animals" cap on over his short bristly grey hair and moved toward his wife for a kiss. The raccoon tail was missing from the back of his cap—it attracted too much attention, he said. That tail was its best feature. I thought it would have looked good right then, flipping left to right, right to left, while he shook his head like that.

My grandfather: at the time of this story, a spry 75-ish Henry Fonda-type. His high-topped leather Red Wing boots gave him a swaggery walk, but he was no John Wayne. His eyes penetrated right into a person; deep, dark blue. The night sky. And inside, a pussycat.

He couldn't put his finger on it at the time, but Poppy told me later that on the drive home that day the car felt like it had been rinsed in emotional apple juice—there was nothing he could touch that wasn't sticky.

Our English family stepped out of the car one at a time: first, Aunt Nana, hair bobbed, no bleach! She had a frenzied intensity, whipped up, empowered with enough adrenaline to wrangle an elk, in a white shirt and khaki pants, red sweater over her shoulder, the sleeves in front with the cuffs turned up together. She was edgy, glistening, not quite sweat, she was way too elegant for sweat, but PO'd at everything and everyone and every star in the galaxy, you could just tell by the hard set of her jaw. Loafers with no socks, but those little sheer footies or peds thingies, erect posture, shoulders squared. Yep, definitely uptight.

Uncle Chuck unfolded slowly out of the front seat, a bit dazed. Fuzzy. He wore dark corduroy pants and a blue pullover shirt, both way too big for him. Had he lost weight? He looked like a ghost. His usually pink English cheeks had pale patches. He hadn't combed his pretty blond hair, and it looked dull, lifeless. His tall lanky body seemed diminished somehow, there was less... light in it.

Then... Jolene. Red hair came first, a great pile of hair, flung out like a wave of Hibiscus blossoms, like rusty red cotton candy with Hibiscus blossoms in it. I don't know. It was amazing.

She stood, frowning, in knee length khaki shorts, sleeveless khaki top and matching sweater thrown casually in a studied sort of way over her shoulders, clasped in front by a gold sweater guard—tiny alligator clamps connected by a thin gold chain; argyle knee socks and Bass Weejun tassel loafers.

A magnificent cross between Pippi Longstocking and a cub scout.

 Tate

I was right! She was a goddess. In knee socks.

And *tassel loafers!*

Into the Middle

Despite the "fight or flight" sparks and jaggy energy oozing out of the Huffingtons' pores, everyone hugged and squeezed and patted each other hello, breaking through the barriers of distance, time, oceans and disillusion.

The adults went up the front steps of the Adobe House: Jock (Poppy) with Maria; Rita with Nana and Fáno, arm in arm, Nana in the middle, a big Nana sandwich with two little pieces of bread; Fox held Chuck's arm, guiding him like a seeing-eye... fox. The Rodriguez family gathered up the groceries and some of the baggage and followed the parade into the house.

We called it the Middle, the living and dining area in the center of the Adobe House. The Middle was spacious, with large blocks of Carmel River stone forming a fireplace that opened through to a matching hearth in Jock & Maria's room on the other side of the east wall. Maria's colorful braided rugs covered the terra cotta Mexican tiles and wide splashes of Peruvian cotton curtains fluttered in the windows. There were leatherback chairs, love seats and a highly polished barn door dining table. Arrowheads and rocks, pictures and odds and ends of memorabilia, the small, artifactual essences of three generations of Wymans, filled window sills and tabletops. Six of Mama Maria's quilts were folded over the rungs of pine ladders on each side of the fireplace.

Jock poured drinks while Maria settled herself into her creaking leather and wicker chair. Felix and Juana and little Chico distributed baggage to the bedrooms and went off to the kitchen to finish up what Rita and they had started for supper: A pot of shredded chicken chili, blue cornbread, butter lettuce salad with Fáno's special vinaigrette and lavender lemonade.

Nana slipped into the small powder room down the hall. She placed her hands on the edge of the sink, leaned over and stared at her reflection in the gold-leafed oval mirror. *I look as tired as I feel*, she thought. She unzipped her khakis and emptied her bladder for the first time since leaving San Francisco. Her sighs pressed against the powder room walls and shoved the available air out of the room. She tucked everything back in, washed her hands (*Ah... lavender soap! I'm home!*) and ran her fingers through her salt & peppery hair.

Just five blissful moments alone, she thought. *No dramas. No long, mournful looks. No sighs. Deep, meaningful sighs. His. Mine. Hers. It doesn't matter.*

Nana joined her parents and sisters and brother-in-law in the Middle and took the goblet of chilled Cold Duck from her father's hand. Jock liked the symmetry of Cold Duck—dregs of red wine mixed with champagne. *Like life,* he thought.

"Where's Chuck?" Nana asked, knowing full well her husband would avoid or ruin every get-together he could from now through eternity. Or until he got a decent job. Or until he left.

Oh, God, she thought. *I hate myself for feeling this way.* She slid onto the pile of pillows in the window seat with a perfect sighting of the Hobbit House. What was that movement out there? The girls? She focused her tired eyes on the late afternoon shadows.

"Wandered off that way," Jock said about Chuck, gesturing down the dark hall to the West Wing of the Adobe House. "Exploring your new rooms, I'd say." Always the diplomat, our Jock.

"Hghmph. Exploring his martini shaker, more like."

Her mother said, "Nana, can we let go of ze problems for ze moment? You're here, Sweetheart, and you're safe. Let Chuck go off and lick his wounds somewhere."

"Oh, Mama, if it were only that basic and simple. But, yes. Of course. You are right. Let's do try to have a jolly evening. It is good to be home. He'll come around, I suppose."

And to herself: *Me too. Maybe.*

 Stevie

We watched our parents and grandparents make their way up the steps to the Adobe, then we cousins sized each other up out of the corners of our six eyes—Jolene's pale blues were knitted close together, bright around the edges, and her hair seemed kind of *on fire* to me. Scorched blossoms. Oooh. Scorched cotton candy and blossoms. I was bedazzled.

Jolene, however, did not share my bedazzlement. My imagination ran amok: I took the look on Jolene's face and turned it into all kinds of disasters. They brewed in my head, like a cup of herbs in hot water.

A squeaky "Hghmph," came from Jolene. I tried to make something out of that, too, but all I could get was, "Hghmph," the sound of a piglet caught in a wire fence.

Tate looked out over the top of Jolene's hair, her navy blue Wyman eyes wary, the whites showing like a nervous, lathered-up pony prepared to bolt.

"Welcome to Sweet Farm." Forced, obviously rehearsed, and ungenerous from the shy pony.

I looked at Jolene, my mind whirling dervishly: Jolene, our old pal. Five years had passed, millions of things had happened and changed in the world, including our own budding little selves, and it was all mixed up in that dervish on a whirl.

Jolene: looking like twenty, feeling like the lost twelve year old she was, along for the ride with crazy parents on the run!

Tate: an under-developed thirteen, a bastard, maybe half-orphan musician.

Me: twelve, going on thirty, looking like ten, with a bit of mystery all tangled up in my braid.

The potential for stories overwhelmed me. So much to talk about. We could tell her all the things we didn't know about Deke, or Fáno; we could sing all the songs Tate wrote for Deke; we could read my latest stories out loud; we could teach her how to make *lembas* bread worthy of any elf! She could tell us about London. Or *her* father!

"C'mon," I said. "Follow us." Tate rolled her eyes. "C'mon!" I rolled mine back and gestured with my head.

And then, being telepathic cousins, after many meaningful stares and nods of the head and sundry other signals to get my point across, Tate received the message.

If Jolene *got* the Hobbit House, if she didn't make fun of it or think it was stupid, well, we would know then that she was our friend, that she belonged. All she had to do was step inside.

"So." I looked at Jolene with my best smile.

"C'mon."

Tate dragged behind only a little.

 Tate

We took several steps before we noticed Jolene had not followed. She was rooted in her tassel loafers by the car, like if she let go of the door handle she would evaporate and there would be nothing left by the car but those shoes and a puff of fairy sprinkles.

We returned to her and said stupid things like, "Are you OK?" and "Did I say something wrong?" She had one hand on the door handle and the other in her hair, trying to brush it out of her eyes and tame it with her fingers, all the time losing a battle against tears.

Stevie and I reached out for Jolene at the same time, but it startled her. She jumped back, like a rabbit, as if we were going to strike her or take aim.

"Blast!" she blurted, and turned away to flee up the Adobe House steps. She let out a little hiccup as she tripped on the woven straw doormat in her tassel loafers.

 Jolene

I just couldn't be nice! I couldn't look at their sweet, happy faces. *Just look at them,* I thought. *The world on a string!*

When I escaped into the house, I side-stepped the adults, deep in conversation about the weather in the Land of Oz, or whatever. Instinct took me to the West Wing, and then I followed my nose to my room, where Juana was putting away my clothes.

Surprised, I stopped at the door, contemplating retreat, but as she looked up and saw my tears, Juana opened her arms. I paused for one split-second, then fell sobbing into her lap. Right then, she *was* my retreat.

I hardly remembered this woman, but there I was, sitting on an American roll-away cot (another cot—will I ever sleep in a real bed again?), folded into her soft Mexican embrace, crying my disenfranchised half-British eyes out.

Juana pulled a wad of tissues out of her apron pocket. She pressed it into my hand and said, "There now, chica. All will be well. Cry until you can cry no more. I will hold you. I will get your mother if you like."

"No! No. I'm so sorry. But, please, don't call Mum. She can't see me crying. I'll pull myself together. Really. I'm all right."

But, I wasn't all right. And Juana knew it. And she knew exactly why. I could see full knowledge of my personal family shame as well as my newly achieved womanhood status written in flashing neon thought bubbles over her head. She got the details, by osmosis, or the sight.

She held me until there were no more tears, until the tissue wad was a soggy mess, until my eyes were red rimmed and I was spent. We didn't talk, really. I learned quickly that even though she knew everything about the Wymans, Juana wasn't much of a talker. She was better at holding.

And she didn't tell me not to cry. I hate it when people say, "Oh don't cry," when it is obviously a situation worthy of many heart-rending tears.

 Stevie

Tate and I watched Jolene stumble up the steps. We thought better of following her.

Disappointed, giving each other the shrug for, "What the heck?" we went into the kitchen to help Felix, Rita and Fáno spread the dinner out on the big table. Deep in thought, I counted out the silverware from its oak box and red checkered cloth napkins from the drawer in the sideboard and set the table while Tate cut the cornbread. Chico sat at the big table in his highchair, munching on a corn dog and gleefully bashing it onto his tray, burbling in his three year old mix of Spanish and English, "Kiss me, por favor, up, up! Steebie! Steebie!" putting his sticky hand out to touch whomever walked near enough. "Cookie? Gracias. Up, up!"

My mind scrambled through a deep thicket of cogitation. I worried that Chuck would make a mess; I considered Nana's peds; I coveted Jolene's alligator clamps, so neatly performing their jobs holding her sweater over her shoulders, even as she flew up the steps in a histrionic flash. I wondered if the tassel loafers were part of her school uniform, and if so, I was so jealous, what with the saddle shoe requirement at Lucia. Saddle shoes. Farley, my friend in Salinas, called them "gunboats."

Not that I really coveted the loafers. They were city girl footwear. But, for a short, stocky girl, anything's better than saddle shoes and white ankle socks. Please! Anything.

I thought about the look on Poppy's face when he blasted free of Cadillac confinement with the three Huffingtons. Disturbance was written all over his face in furrows and creases. A little dark cloud hung around his head.

I considered the wonderment of Jolene's breasts. I looked down at my own chest—two little marbles in a training bra. Tate was so flat she didn't even wear a bra, and she was the oldest. Oh, she was going to hate this. I considered the injustice of it, and imagined the fantastic awkwardness when we first undressed in each other's presence, which was bound to happen.

I was contemplating whether or not I'd see Jolene again this night, when Juana came in, patted her little one on the head and spoke softly to Rita, who, in her perfect wisdom and soothing Glinda-Good-Witch-of-the-North voice, said, "Leave her be, then. I'll take her something later. It's been a big day."

Excerpt from Stevie's Honors English Journal 1960s
The Parents

My mother, Rita Grace Wyman (born September 25, 1925, Libra) met my father, Stefáno "Fáno" Michel (born December 25, 1920, Capricorn) in the Pitié-Salpêtrière Hospital in Paris in January 1948. She was a nurses' aid studying French and, well, all I know for sure is that he was in need of some aid from a nurse. And spoke French.

She gave him aid, but it got her fired and him, uhm, better! They married and I was already hitchhiking a ride in her womb when they left Paris for Carmel. I've seen the pictures. Definitely me in there.

Rita came home with three new things: a mystified half-French husband, Fáno; the tiny bun that would be me baking in her personal oven; and a precious copy of the 1937 UK edition of The Hobbit, given to her by a grateful patient, which would prove to be a great source of inspiration.

They don't talk about it, but I think Mama Maria didn't much take to Fáno for about three months.

"Tzigani," she whispered, amazed. People who think of themselves as displaced French aristocrats tend to look down their noses at the French Romani. "Tzigani" is pronounced with a kind of hisssss and a spit, Tzzzzigáaani. It is not a compliment.

And all Rita could reply was, "Yes, yes, he really is, Mama." She told me all this in a whisper.

Or Fáno, "Oui, Mama Maria, I am theez wild man. Yes. Eet eez true eenough." With that glorious smile, his small, even white teeth glinting and sparking, dimpled cheeks twitching, blacker-than-night curls bobbing, he was completely unphased by his new mother-in-law's cold shoulder. He knew the ice would melt.

August 1960

Sweet Farm
Dinner and Other Complications

Chuck emerged for dinner from his hidey-hole in their bedroom, filled a ceramic bowl with a spoonful of chili, broke two pieces of Juana's precious, award-winning blue cornbread into it and then did not touch his food again—just sat at the far end of the table gazing into the bowl as if it held the hope of the future: a scrying chili bowl. Aunt Nana sat at the other end of the table, as far away as she could get and still be at dinner. She scraped little bits of undressed lettuce around on her plate with a fork and looked at the floor.

We were all seated: the Wymans, the Michels, the Huffingtons and the Rodriguezes, the whole extended family except the always-conspicuous-by-his-many-year-AWOL, Deke, and Jolene, who, Rita quickly explained, was "lying down for a bit."

Jock considered this, then raised his glass, looked at his middle daughter and said, finally, "Blessings on this food and our family. Welcome Home, Noonie."

Tears welled in Nana's eyes at the sound of her nickname, but she was not about to break down, not in front of Charles, anyway. She could jolly well hold out forever.

Chuck woke the next morning at 6 in a fetal position on the cold tile floor in the corner of the bedroom he newly shared with Nana in the West Wing. He was wrapped in a scratchy wool blanket, wearing only pajama tops and white socks scrunched down around his never-seen-the-sun ankles.

Disoriented, Chuck thought he was in his bedroom at his mother, Lady Charlotte's flat in London, until he looked over and saw the sleeping Nana, in pink & white polka-dotted pajamas, curled up on her side, draped over the mattress edge of the pineapple four-poster bed in her childhood room.

She mumbled in her sleep, something about "chocolate houses need peppermint lawns," or "dawns," or "songs." He couldn't tell. She turned over toward the center of the bed.

Right, then. We are at Sweet Farm.

The few functional synapses in Charles's soaked brain contemplated the sleeping Nana, his wife of 14 years. *My rock. My center of the universe,* he thought, each word percussing against the side of his head.

Each word a lie.

Sisters

Stevie and Tate were asleep in Stevie's room, dead to the world on the double bed in short pajamas and tangled blankets.

Jolene huddled in her borrowed cot, wide awake, 5,371 miles away from everything she knew and loved and all her friends, with a body suddenly grown up before she was quite prepared. Oh, and frozen, non-speaking-to-each-other, whacko parents.

Maria and Jock, well, they were fine, ensconced on their bed in the East Wing, steaming cups of coffee on their bedside tables and the Sunday San Francisco *Chronicle* Pink Sheet and Comics spread out on the quilt; Jock reading Herb Caen; Maria, *Life Styles*.

In the West Wing bathroom, Chuck found his pajama bottoms and pulled them on, took five aspirin out of the medicine cabinet above the sink and popped them in his mouth, splashed a short snort of gin from his paper-sleeved bottle not-so-hidden under the sink into a water glass, tossed it back and followed it with a chaser of warm water that shot from the tap into the glass with a noisy shudder and a rusty splash. He stared at the rust in the sink.

Shambling across the hall, he slipped on the braided floor runner and bashed his head on the door jamb. Holding his head onto his shoulders with one hand, Chuck gripped the headboard with the other as he got into the bed. He noticed that his side had not been slept in, pillow not used. *How did I end up on the floor? And now, where is Nana?*

The compound was quiet. No one had made a plan for this sisterly assignation, but each knew upon awakening that the others were waiting.

Now, 7am on Sunday morning, Rita, Nana and Fox sat in pajamas at the Formica counter in Rita's kitchen in the Chapel House, sipping dense black coffee and nibbling warm lemon scones with thick raspberry jam and soft unsalted butter. They could see Fáno through the kitchen window, strolling between the rows of blooming lavender bushes, his arms outstretched and hands open, fingertips kissing the tops of the papery blossoms, his dark skin absorbing the fine and tranquilizing essence of lavender.

Rita's kitchen counter had been a gathering place for the sisters for twelve years, since Fáno had remodeled the old chapel/bunkhouse on the Sweet Farm compound for their little home.

Nana described the day before. "And there he sat: a mummy, a rag doll, like he was dead. He hardly spoke all day, at least not to me, but then, I can't blame him for that, there being no room for words, what with the ELEPHANTS UNDER EVERY RUG! And poor Jolene. I accidentally spilled the beans about her money and..."

"Her money? You mean her college fund from Poppy and Mama? I thought that was sacred?" Fox's nose was twitching.

"Yes, right. It's odd, really, I thought that living in England would help settle Chuck, make him feel more at peace, get him better gigs, in his own country and all. I thought his mother's support would help, although it's stifling, at times. He always seemed to feel out of place here. But he is out of place everywhere. Oh! I don't know why we came home. Yes, I do! We are broke and have been chucked out of our flat! Thank God Poppy wired us money for the plane tickets, or we'd be in the street. Lovely for Jolene."

"You'd never be in the street, you know. But, anyway, what's he going to do, Noonie? He has no other skills, obviously, and..."

"Yeah, thanks for the reminder. And he's not that charming a pianist anymore, because he never practices and his moodiness is driving audiences away, and me? Crazy! He plays the same old rut stuff, just to get through the night. He wanders around with his conductor's baton gripped in his hand like a lifeline, like it attaches him to the stupid Super Conductor, even though he has no engagements lined up. He's lost whatever edge he had. I don't know what he'll do, or what we'll do. It was hard enough to get onto a plane and out of England. Lady Charlotte was no help at all. She had a fit we were leaving. She kept saying we needed to stay near her. That it was important. At the same time, she kept giving us things. Books. Photos."

"Well, at least you can start Jolene at Lucia with Tate and Stevie in September. They're doing well enough there." Fox liked to have answers.

"Nice idea, but Santa Lucia costs money, which we do not have, and I am not asking Poppy and Mama to pay for it. Principles, I guess."

"Principles, shminciples," Fox said. "Jolene needs to be with her cousins. Poppy and Mama want to do it. They think it's their right as grandparents."

"Chuck will have a fit, Fox. And what do you think Mama and Poppy will say when they hear he's gone through Jolene's money, too, not to mention basically ruining my job with Croft & Anderson?" She thought about that while she scraped some butter off her scone. "Yeah. He has a tiny bit of pride left, miniscule, gnat-sized, tucked somewhere inside his crazy mind, and I can't imagine he'll sit still, drunk or sober, high or low, for another handout from my family. At least not without a royal British scene."

"Ah," said Rita. "You have it right there! Family! We will take care of each other. That's what families do!"

"Baloney. Chuck is my so-called family, and he's done nothing but screw things up for 14 years. He's so unpredictable. He went to the bank without me, to answer that question still hanging in the air, Fox, about Jolene's college fund? I made all our accounts "either/or," if you get my drift. Shouldn't have. While I wasn't watching, Chuck took out money in snippets, always planning to put it back, of course, after he made a million pounds, when he became famous. Which, of course, never materialized. And never will. Who could handle him? So, before I knew it, everything was gone, except for the small account I kept for groceries and basics, about 300 pounds. I paid off the landlord with that—for the door Chuck kicked in the night he exploded."

"Tell us about that, honey." Rita stirred cream into her coffee, looking at her sisters. She knew she was lucky with Fáno, and it could have gone so differently. Hard to believe that the one stable male of the three was her husband, little Fáno, the one with no education, no family and a large dose of so-called undesirable blood. All that, and he was solid as a rock.

"Ah, God. Chuck came home that night all liquored up, I could tell something had gone terribly wrong. He has a little tick in his left eye that twitches when he is upset or on the verge. He was sweaty, big dark rings of sweat under his arms, and he seemed more drunk than usual, more out of control. He stank. His eyes were... weird. It spilled all over me, like sand and kelp washing over rocks in the surf at the beach.

"He was in a panic, describing it like a movie: being cultivated, no—more like, rushed, by this man, Guy Templeton, some London real estate investment banker shyster person who sweet-talked Chuck and that worthless Steven Barrymore or whatever, Barrington, I can't think, into this deal. And then another deal. And debt! All focused on Chuck's future as a musician, as a star, a commodity. He started to believe his own Super Conductor story. He got so puffed up. It was pitiful. Non-refundable deposits made on air, clouds, naive ego. One crazy person's imagination. A drunk's fantasy.

"And then, well, then this Guy Templeton split, dumped them, took the money out of their business account and left the country. I guess he realized he had gotten all he could from the situation, got wind of *the reality of Chuck*, maybe, so he left them with debt and cream pie splat in their faces—this is what I think, anyway, I never talked to the man myself, the Huffington wives don't do that, get too involved, but I know... I know that Chuck... I know that..."

Nana's eyes filled with tears.

"We know, honey. We know." Across the gold-flecked counter, Rita took her sister's hand, and Fox took the other.

Through her now flowing tears, Nana said, "And then, he exploded. Like a cannon; a combustible engine that could suddenly take no more pressure; a balloon filled with venom. He pounded the walls and kicked at the door, which splintered."

"Did he hurt you?" Rita trembled at the thought of the scene.

"No, no. His hatred was all for himself... and the door." Nana exhaled.

Chuck: a drink in one hand, a cigarette in the other, sitting at the piano, doodling out dark songs. The darling, talented, reluctant young Lord one minute, the dark and evil twin the next.

How the beautiful, brilliant, glorious and statuesque Nana Wyman (in school she was known as the Hanger—her shoulders were so straight across, she could wear a belted flour sack and look like a million)—how she got mixed up in Charles Huffington's crazy shenanigans, no one knew. Nana barely knew. That time, that feeling, that heart elation, was gone.

She could remember the music, the dance, the starry night, the fragrance of gardenias, and then...

What Nana knew now was that there was Jolene. Jolene needed her father. And Jolene deserved better than this.

Moving into the West Wing of the Adobe House at the corner of Carmel Valley and Schulte Roads was a snap for the Huffingtons, what with no furniture and all.

Jolene stayed in her room, buried in blankets, hugging a hot water bottle. Jolene's head throbbed, her tummy hurt and her feelings were a-jumble. The stress of the day before, perhaps the weeks before (just think what Jolene heard, saw and contemplated as her parents' world collapsed) was slowly ebbing out of her body, sigh by sigh. She burrowed further under the covers, pulled her bedraggled stuffed rabbit close for comfort, put the pillow over her head, and thought about all the plans she had made for August—dashed now by drama.

Nana, scowling, put away her clothes, such as they were, she didn't have time or room to pack anything but country essentials: faded jeans, shirts (two denim, one plaid), boots, socks, her favorite straw hat, a couple of sweaters, the ubiquitous khakis. Mara, her friend in the apartment next door in London, had piled Nana's remaining non-essential skirts, business suits and high heels into her guest room, telling Nana to cable with shipping instructions. Good neighbor, she eventually stashed it all in several boxes marked "Huff," which she stored in the closet. Who knew when Nana would be in touch?

Nana thought, *What I need is a job. Something to get me out of here on a daily basis. If I have to bump into Chuck all day, see that mournful face, I'll go insane. I'll kill him.*

Nana's mind was playing tricks on her today. One minute she was full of anger, hardly standing the sight of her husband. He had ruined their lives.

And then, she brimmed with remorse and guilt, feeling sorry for him, hoping *her* secrets could stay under wraps.

Where is Chuck, anyway? He can put away his own blasted clothes.

Excerpt from Stevie's Honors English journal 1960s
My World

Sweet Farm & Lavandula & the Sweet Tea Room are tied up like the laces on my Converse tennis shoes, so if you want to know about my mother, and the Tea Room, you get Sweet Farm, too. And Lavandula. And my amazing grandmother.

My grandfather, Jock Wyman, Poppy, retired in 1940 from Case Western Reserve in Hudson, Ohio, after 20 years of teaching American Lit and living in a faculty house just off campus. The way he tells it, for the entire 20 years he had indigestion, a perpetual frown and a fear of dust, libraries and men's toilet stalls. He showed me his little notebook calculations: he spent 3200 days, or 25,600 hours, or 1,536,000 minutes, or 92,160,000 seconds teaching. And during each of those days, hours, minutes or seconds, he was nervous and wanted to throw up.

One day, he thought, "Maybe it's me."

Duh.

It took him a score of years to figure out that he was terrified of teaching. He bore no ill-will toward his students: they were brilliant, the cream of the crop, he was fortunate to be there among them and his fellow professors. His ill-will was toward himself, for failure as a don of letters—he thought he would think more *of it. He thought he would love doing it. He surely didn't think he'd be throwing up in the men's room before class.*

He loved his subject: romping around in the field of dreams with Whitman, Emerson, Hemingway. Sinclair Lewis. He was really up on depression era writers: John Steinbeck, Henry Miller.

My grandmother, Maria, when finally told this private thing, was French cool. She asked him, if he could retire right now and do anything he wanted, what would he do?

He pondered this for a moment before he answered. He thought it might be a loaded question. She had that loaded look in her eye, the Gimlet, he called it, sort of a flinty, squinty thing. He told her, he thought if he could really do anything, he would begin a literary and geographical quest by "looking for John Steinbeck." He never thought he'd meet him, he just wanted to explore the wild and beautiful countryside in which Mr. Steinbeck grew up and wrote about: the Pinnacles, King City, Carmel Valley, the Pacific Ocean, tide pools on the rocks and beaches of Monterey Bay.

Poppy's hobby is everything John Steinbeck. He gives Steinbeck pop quizzes to his family.

Him: "Who were Cain and Abel?"

Us: "In a story in Genesis in the Bible, but also the names Adam Trask almost gave his twin sons, but after a long philosophical discussion, decided instead to call them Caleb and Aaron. In East of Eden.*"*

You have to give complete answers or, if he's in his study, he rings this little bell.

So, they sold most of their stuff, really, and packed minimal belongings—two small suitcases apiece—and took the train from Cleveland to San Francisco: four days in a sleeping car, some food in a hamper, a few meals in the dining car that was six wobbly, shaking cars away from their little home on the rails. No hotel reservations on ar-  *rival, no nothing. A 55-year-old man, his restless, hot-to-go-somewhere 45-year-old Americanized French wife, and three daughters, Rita, 15, Nana, 12, and Fox,10, a small suitcase apiece and a straw katie-boater, the hat of the season, each with a wide colored ribbon: pink, yellow, blue.*

Mama Maria's early retirement gift to Poppy was California. Not a visit, but a new life, and a secret savings account.

She told me that back then she was sick of being in the same old place for 20 years (Hudson, Ohio) lovely as it was, crocheting doilies and serving endless cups of tea to other faculty wives, and was full-on-busting ready, well, my phrase, not hers, to go somewhere new with Jock. She had no idea he was throwing up in the men's room.

"He zhould have been an actor," she said, accented in her indelible French.

Ha! She should have been an actress! She had this bank roll and never told anyone!

"Eet just never came up," she shrugged.

She's crafty, our grandmother. There are afghans and braided rugs in our houses that she's made from scraps of our old clothes blended with odds and ends from the thrift shop. And the quilts!

In Lavandula, she's got fabric and supplies for every kind of sewing and quilting, candle and soap molds, flower presses and colored pencils, yarns and embroidery thread, a distillery for lavender and herbs. But I am getting ahead of myself.

In 1940, she figured she could do her thing anywhere—she was just ready to get out of Dodge (Hudson). Jock was too old to be called to war, she had three daughters to rear, and so she proposed to buy some "little place" near or in Salinas. Poppy could follow his nose and she could set up a studio to make her stuff. She heard that the schools were good "out there in California."

August 1960

The Sweet Farm office
A Job For Chuck

Where Chuck was, while Nana was grumbling and unpacking her twelve articles of clothing in the West Wing, was in a 5 x 25 foot room, a long, thin slice of lavender space: the Sweet Farm office. With a door at each end, each with a glass window, the only natural light in the room save for a small leaky skylight, the room ran the full width down the center of the barn, which was otherwise divided loosely into quarters. On one side were Fox and Tate's apartment in the back and the Sweet Tea Room in front. On the other, Lavandula in front, the Distillery in back.

Along the west wall, the office furniture included 3 tall black metal file cabinets (one for the farm, one for Sweet Tea, one for Lavandula), a long, skinny drawing table, lamp and stool, racks and racks of sketches, labels, paper bags, small jars, and other sundries for the Sweet Farm research and development department, an over-sized mahogany desk from whose exposed corners Fox had permanent upper thigh bruises, a desk chair and two little folding chairs for occasional visitors. There wasn't much room in there.

But there they sat, Charles Huffington and Fox Wyman, scrunched into the two folding chairs, knee to knee.

She figured she'd better offer him a job, keep control of the impending collision of Chuck, Sweet Farm and her sister. She could see right off there was no problem re: who's boss. They were a collective mess, those Huffingtons.

"What on earth would I do, Fox?" Chuck interrupted her brief reverie. "Trot your mail to the Post Office? Take orders from Felix in the fields? Fáno in the Distillery? I think not, sister-in-law."

"C'mon, Charles. There's millions of things to do: orders, billing, packaging. We're about to harvest and distill the lavender; we have holiday orders coming in already; Rita's up to her eyeballs in flour, sugar and butter over there in the Tea Room and thinking up new menu items all the time. Why, it's enough of a job keeping a cap on her bottle of ideas! We've grown fast. We need you. We'll find the right niche for you. Promise. The point is that this is a family business, and, well, you need something to do, so why not help me? I am on overwhelm most of the time. It would be good to fit you in here, take some of the load off."

Chuck looked at Fox skeptically. He didn't trust the sly Fox. He though she had x-ray vision, maybe it was the fox-ish amber eyes and rusted hair. Maybe it was her too apt name: she was witchy, and could see through him and into his soul, where all the bad stuff lay hidden behind rocks in the cave of his self doubt.

It gave him gooseflesh. He felt exposed, unstable, vulnerable. *Work for her?*

"No."

"Why ever *not*, Charles? We need help, you're here. I imagine you'll need some time to re-group, you know, from your... disappointments and all. So, help *me*. Believe me, there's plenty of time to be in your own thoughts while you're trimming lavender. It will satisfy the room and board requirement we all fulfill and give you some cash besides. It's not a comedown, Chuck. Just think of it as a..." (she was about to say *holiday*, but that seemed disingenuous). "Think about it, anyway. It's not, uhm, like you have a lot of options."

Oh dear. That put my foot in, Fox thought, watching Chuck's face crumble into a hundred puzzle pieces. She wondered if he fortified himself for this meeting with a quick shot. *Yes, of course. If I were Chuck, I'd've had a couple of glugs of gin, straight from the bottle. Definitely.*

Pretty soon, Chuck would not be able to breathe under this blanket of disgrace. He looked at Fox, well, more... through her: she disappeared from his sight, his eyes wandered out the open back door to the rows of lavender plants, merrily waving tissuey blossoms in the coastal breeze. His mind moved to the door and his body got up and followed. He stepped out, walked down the dirt path to Schulte Road and turned right. He did not look back or say goodbye to Fox.

This is so absolutely insane, he thought. *There is no way in hell I'd ever work for you, Fox Wyman. Work for you, indeed.*

This place owns you, and I won't let that happen to me. No sirree Bob, I'll park cars before I'll be under your spell; sell insurance; wait tables. Live with my mother! Anything but do your bidding at Sweet Farm. No, no.

Chuck trudged down the road to a quiet spot under the Schulte Road Bridge, where there were "lions and tigers and bears," according to the young cousins.

He scrambled down the bank, through foxtails and stickers that clung to his pants and socks, found his little hollow in a pile of boulders, protected all around with scrub oak and willows, tucked in behind the concrete pilings, close enough to the farm that he could walk to it and far enough away that no one ever came to look for him. When he came back, he just said, "I've been for a walk."

Fox watched Chuck's defeated form as he walked out the door. She sighed. A deep, sorry, empathic sigh. *Ah, Chuck, you old sot. I must be crazy, even if you wanted this job, which you don't, which you won't, which you can't.*

Fox got up from her little chair, ran her fingers through her fine, straight, bobbed coppery hair that naturally flipped up in a sort of L on the ends, sighed again, walked to the door, stepped outside and breathed deeply the lavender-scented air. She slipped in the door to the right, into the Tea Room, where she found Rita, alone in the pantry, counting out muffin tin liners. Fox could see Fáno out front, his head bent over a tomato plant so laden with fruit that his earlier stakes had failed, and he was replacing them, gently pulling the vines out of the way.

Fox felt awkward sometimes around Rita and Fáno's happiness. Surrounded as she was by her family, she was desert island lonely. She had few friends, except her sisters. There was no man for her, hadn't been anyone since Deke. It was scary, and she was too fragile to fall in love. Too busy. Besides, she did not trust her taste in men.

There had been one mild flirtation—that hunky lavender farmer, Michael Bossard from Mendocino who stopped by Sweet Farm one day as he drove out Carmel Valley Road. He came back twice, took her to dinner at Abalonetti's on the Wharf in Monterey and fed her seafood gumbo, warm garlic bread and chilled chablis. They went to Carmel and walked the Main Beach at the end of Ocean Avenue all the way to the Frank Lloyd Wright house where the kelp piled up in aromatic mounds and spread long, slender fingers across the wet sand. They took off their shoes and kelp bulbs squeaked and popped under their feet. Michael was sweet, and when he bent to kiss her, it freaked her out so badly that she bolted barefooted back to the car and hugged the door all the way home.

That was the end of that. She just couldn't explain.

And Joe Bartlett, but he didn't count: they'd known each other since childhood and had discovered the thrill of bodies pressed together under the blankets in his bed when they were 11. Their occasional "lunches" were mildly satisfying: picnics up on the Laureles Grade under the white oaks; an hour "picking wildflowers" along Tassajara Road on a hot valley day. But that was nothing.

And the knowledge of that, the nothingness of it, the fact that there was no bed for it, no sacred space, just deepened her aloneness.

After Deke disappeared, no way would she put herself in that position again. Ho, no. Between the humiliation and the fear, the tears and the pain, she didn't know which was worse.

Tate was too young to really understand the empty space he left in their lives. But, Fox? She felt the slap in the face, every day. Was she that horrible a person that someone could just walk away, disappear without a trace, no note, no forwarding address, no hint? Was Deke's life with her so awful that he could just turn his back on his daughter, drive away, abandon the Sweet Farm truck, out of gas, in a ravine and, what? Change his name? Leave the country? If so, how did he do it? Was he just done with the commitment? "Bye bye, Fox and Tate. Nice knowin' ya!" Really?

The day after they'd determined that he was not carousing with cowboys, since none of the usual cowboy mates copped to having seen him before, during or after the Rodeo, after she spent all her tears and recriminations like change at the dime store, she found his wallet on the floor by the dresser on her way to bed. His wallet! How far could he have gotten without his wallet? In it: his driver's license, $52, a picture of Tate in red flannel pajamas sitting on the rug in front of the 1949 Wyman family Christmas tree, and a folded note Fox slipped under his door after their first night in the bunkhouse: *More, Fox.*

Every day since the summer of 1950, her thoughts eventually ran to Deke. Was he dead? Married? Should I have married him? It was a sore spot with Jock and Maria. "That girl needs her father's name!"

Why? Dammit. Why did he leave, why did that happen? I thought we were OK. Fox found herself tallying, the way her father did at Case. Just this July, when she got to 10 years or 3,653 days since Deke left her at the Rodeo grounds, she made herself quit counting.

Chuck reached his rock, and sat down. Ahhh, the rock. *The rock.* He felt around for his flask behind the boulders, nestled in the weeds. He uncapped the gin and drank deeply, wiped his mouth on the cuff of his shirt, recapped the flask and put it back.

His new rule: Always return the flask to its hiding place between drinks. Such a lovely hiding place, tucked as it was in the weeds.

Chuck sat on his rock, ruminating. *What else is there to do?* he asks. *I am treading water. There is no purpose, no focus. No Nana. No charm. What is there, really? Jolene, but she doesn't need me. She would be better off without me, surely. What is the point to all this?*

Work for Fox? I'd rather die. I am an artist, a musician. The Super Conductor! Not to mention a bloody stupid Lord. Look at these hands. Artist's hands. La-di-da Lordly hands. Need gloves. Need sleep. Oh, what in blazes am I doing and when will it stop? Don't know. Oh, I do know. But I need sleep. Need some peace.

No. I won't work for her. She's too hot. No. She's too... she's too... hard. Orange. She's very... orange. And those amber eyes.

1946

Salinas, California
Dunes of Dust

When Deke Harley rumbled southwest off the highway and pulled his 1940 turquoise Indian Chief into downtown Salinas in 1946, the taste of Cimarron County dust still lingered in his mouth. His jeans were stiff and bleached with the dry blood color of it, his eyes burnt from the floury grit. The red dust that slapped on and stuck to the bike left a smear of purple: sometimes red and blue make bruise. Even four years in the Army could not erase the flavor of Oklahoma dust on Deke's tongue. It was an unwelcome spice at every meal. A part of him. 10 years of dust in the face and mouth and ears and hair and clothes and lungs and skin, never leave a man. Those were some hard years for Oklahoma.

He sat on the bike and looked up Main Street. In the back of his mind, though, his mother, Rebecca, was saying goodbye to her son again and he was itching to get on the road—two months after his discharge from the Army. They sat in the little trailer in Cimarron, drinking tea in tin cups. Rebecca's dress, Deke noted, once bright pink, had turned to ashes of roses, bleached out from relentless sun, pockets and cuffs frayed. It fell on her thin bones like an empty pillowcase pinned to a clothesline. Rebecca's once lustrous blonde hair was pulled back in a severe bun. One of her spectacles was cracked; her hands were chapped, her wedding ring missing.

"I can't stay here, Ma. This place. It gives me the heebies. I'll find us somethin' better."

This place was a tiny trailer parked next to Rebecca's sister-in-law, Pru's one room cabin, perched on another dune of dust. That cabin was what Prudence managed to hold onto after the untimely demise of *her* husband, Willard Harley, Deke's uncle. Willard's orneriness had put him in direct harm's way of a tractor: one of the giant mechanical soulless eight-wheeled insects, sent from Hell by the Devil to consume the state of Oklahoma and mow down his, Willard's home, his land.

As he lay suffering from wounds received in the moment of folly called "defending his property," which had been bought out from under him by the driver of the mechanical giant in question, Willard knew it was a psychopathic monster driving these machines: a manic, frenzied, greedy, hungry monster named AGRO, whose many course dinner was in *his*, Willard's fields. But there was nothing he could do. They plowed 24 hours a day. They owned him.

And he died.

Soon after Willard's death, a desperate Prudence took up with a Choctaw farrier, whose main goal in life was to stay pickled around the clock on home-cooked White Lightning, not to sift dust and shore up posts. He had horses to shoe and a brew to sell!

The little trailer was all Rebecca had left of the Harley Farm. Rebecca didn't like it either, but where else could she go? Without Hiram, Deke's father, or Deke, for that matter, she was useless on the old farm, what was left of it. There hadn't been enough money even when Hiram was still alive to dig the shed out from under the dust—they just kept scooping it away at the front and made a kind of tunnel to the door. Each scoop of dust just stirred up more dust, so why bother? It was life down a rabbit hole. A dry rabbit hole.

Over the years, after the rains came back a little, the wild grasses grew again, but the Harleys paid it no mind. Hiram and Rebecca just kept on trudging through the chores: dig furrows, sow seeds, scrape the dunes, hack off the trailing roots of the prairie grasses that dangled through ceilings and crept into the cracks in the walls.

One day 40 year old Hiram fell over dead of a heart attack while shimmying down the well for a dropped bucket. Deke and his mother had a hard time getting Hiram out and considered just filling in the well as a kind of monument to the tough life of Hiram Harley, but, even as low as the water was, that seemed frivolous, so they enlisted a friendly neighbor with a team of mules, who roped Hiram's body and tugged and scraped him up the walls of the well to deposit him with a thump on the hard, dusty ground. By then, Hiram's dead, wet body was nothing pretty to look at.

After they put Hiram to rest in the great burial dune, Deke did his best to prop things up at Harley Farm, but Rebecca's heart wasn't in it now, and Deke's had never been. The last cow was dry, the crop hardly worth calling beans, the soil slow to recover in the driest, dustiest, poorest, most out of the way neck of the woods tucked into the panhandle of Oklahoma.

And then, young Hi died, coughing up blood and the last remnants of the dust pneumonia which had plagued his skinny, tender body for years. The boy suffered long hours of coughing fits and shivered through many nights. His mother watched him disintegrate, day by day. She sponged his feverish head, wrapped his trembling body in warm blankets, fed him bone broth and bread soaked in warm clabber, and finally, held his hand, when she knew that all her ministrations were of no further use. After that, Rebecca's spirit deflated like a party balloon.

In the spring of 1942, Deke opened a nice letter from Uncle Sam, in need of his services.

Deke had six weeks and about $50 to deal with things at home before going off to protect England and France from the ravages of war. Moving his mom's trailer next to Prudence's cabin seemed like the right thing to do at the time, at least the most convenient, but it was soon clear by Rebecca's letters that things were not entirely copacetic on the Oklahoma front.

Dear Son,

I miss you, and Hiram, and little Hi. I miss them more, you know, since I will never see them again, but I worry over you all the time. Will a shell strike you down to leave me all alone in this sorry world? For I am alone, for all that I live side by side with Pru and her Indian, Jon Redbird. His is a dissipate nature—he squanders his time and what little money he earns as a farrier on his still, which is a poor business.

I have obtained work as a laundress in the home of the Bostocks—a slippery downhill slide from my hours of higher learning at my daddy's knee in the library at Snippet

Sound, I know. But, there is no place for an educated Maryland woman here, at least for now; no one cares, they are busy surviving and digging out of this bowl of dust, believing things are getting better. Washing other people's dirty socks puts food on our shared table, as long as I get provisions before Jon Redbird hears the coins jingling in my pocket. So there you have it. Life plods along here, like Gert, the old dray horse at the Sound. I wonder if she is still alive?

Be well and be safe, Rebecca

Deke worried about his mother while she was concerned about him. He could take care of himself. Could she? He wired all the money he could, but it was never enough. His mother, doing laundry!

Dear Son,

Thank you for the money, once again. It enabled me to put some curtains on my trailer windows.

She was too stubborn to write her father, old Judge Harris, for help. She'd die in poverty and disgrace before she'd let him say, "I told you so." She would not hear one word against Hiram Harley or his dreams of western farming gone to hell.

Maybe he, Deke, should get in touch with the Judge, introduce himself, eat crow for his mother's sake and get her some financial aid, go to Maryland and find him. But, no, she would never forgive him for that. She'll go to her grave sooner or later and her pride will get buried along with her precious family Bible and the famous pearls with the diamond clasp, the ones her mother, Mrs. Judge Harris, secretly slipped into the pocket of the 18 year old Rebecca's apron on the eve of her departure for Oklahoma in 1923.

"You might need these," her mother whispered in her ear.

"I won't be going to the opera in Cimarron County, Mother," her daughter replied, fingering the double strand of pearls with her warm hand.

"Even so, Becca." Her mother knew, if Rebecca didn't, that the prospects of her being truly happy in a place called No Man's Land were slim at best. The pearls could be her salvation, her escape. It was the only thing of value she took with her: that, the leatherbound Bible and her innocence, which was duly sacrificed three weeks later on a straw mattress in a "temporary" shed. From then on, her eyes were wide open.

Hiram had been lured to the Oklahoma panhandle by speculators and suitcase bankers with promises of green and bountiful farming in a Garden of Eden. They brokered deals and went back to their safe cities with fat wads of cash and a chuckle or two to share with their drinking buddies down at the tavern about gullible people with ready funds.

Turned out that shed was their home. Their *home* home. Hiram, after adding on a lean-to and an outhouse and a cook shed, each eventually connected by tunnels of dune dust,

74

called that ersatz compound their *home*. Rebecca never called it anything but the *shed*. An then *the sheds*. Even the trailer was just another *shed*.

The rain stopped in 1931, the winds blew up to 100 miles an hour and just wiped away the surface of the earth. By 1933, not only the shed(s), but the other little buildings in the neighborhood thrown up in haste and determination by Hiram and a few rugged pioneer spirits, were bathed in a powdery red dust and the crops of beans and corn were fried to a crisp by the electromagnetic sizzle in the air. All of Hiram's wild dreams were zapped. He wasn't a big conglomerate farmer, squeezing the richness out of the land, but he'd done his share of stripping the soil of its sustaining grasses, so no, he was not entirely guilt free.

But this isn't Hiram's story.

August 1960

Sweet Farm

Chuck Dreams and Fox Remembers

The Super Conductor flew high above the clouds: tiny fingers of cool blue air touched his face, caressed him, fondled his cheeks and fluttered gently through his hair. His arms stretched out, magic wand in hand, zapping the air with tiny bolts of blue, his legs straight but fluid, forming his body into a perfect flying cross. He wore white, floaty clothes, an angelic tuxedo, which cupped the soft air like wings. His hair was golden, his head haloed and glowing with light. He felt at peace, wonderful, like there was not a problem in the world, he was a fleck in the Creator's beautiful, all loving, all encompassing eye.

He awoke with a start, his usual morning headache suddenly and ferociously penetrating from his cranium down to his toes, immobilizing, holding his head down to the pillow as if weighted with bricks. He lay still as stone, on his back, staring at the ceiling. It would be so nice if he could just float, forever...

On the other side of the Sweet Farm compound, Fox awoke about the same time Chuck was lying flat on his bed with his eyes locked on the imaginary blue sky spread out above him, wishing he were anywhere but here.

It was Saturday, and Fox had a tour of the farm to give to a group of Ag students from Salinas; some Sweet Farm gifts to wrap; cucumber & lavender lemonade to make with Rita for the above group tour: *ah, yes, do that first;* and a 3pm visit from Virginia Smith from the local paper, the *Acorn*, to talk about Sweet Farm and what goes on in a typical day.

That's a laugh, she thought. *What goes on in a day. A lot more than growing lavender.*

Fox turned over in her bed toward the little oak side table and opened the drawer, dug down beneath the #2 pencils, the body lotion, Deke's old Chinese bamboo back scratcher and the half empty bottle of aspirin, and brought out the small polaroid of Deke, the only remaining photo she knew of, which she kept hidden from Tate, and, in fact, from everyone on Sweet Farm, all of whom assumed she was bitter and finished, had wiped Deke off her list like so much chalk from the blackboard.

This was not true. The faded black and white photo was worn with worry, fried on the edges and curled up, browned from the lavender and herb oils which clung to Fox's finger-tips. In the picture, Deke leaned against the side of the barn, finished in the lavender fields for the day. He looked at the orange-haired girl behind the camera with longing. She always smiled when she first saw that look in the photo, just for a mo-ment. Because, she always cried, too. He wore jeans, endear-ingly too long, rolled up at the cuffs, showing plaid flannel at the bottom. His T shirt, tight across his muscular chest, was dusted, as was everything, with the powdery scent of lavender.

"A lot better'n red dust, Baby. No problem, **a**tall," Deke said just before she snapped the photo. His cigarette curled smoke up toward the eaves of the barn and spread out flat, dispersing over his blonde head and surrounding his cheeky grin, then poofing away. Even in black and white, he looked so alive, he couldn't be dead.

Fox carefully put the faded polaroid photo away and threw back the four layers of colorful quilts, ready to go about her business. As she swung her feet off the bed and pulled on her knitted slipper-socks, a picture of the moment they met popped into her mind: outside the farm gate in 1946, when Deke came to apply for the manager's job.

He sat on his turquoise bike at the end of the driveway, thinking about coming in. She was just home from her summer school teacher's aid job and the woman with whom she rode to work, Daisy Johnson, had dropped her off at the head of Schulte Road. Fox's yellow checked shirtwaist dress had a small dark red stain on the front from the cafeteria meatball sauce.

She approached the broad back of Deke Harley, in black leather from neck to waist, jeans a long way down to high-topped boots. He was perched on the seat of his motorcycle by the driveway, head down, reading something, a clipping or piece of paper. He turned his head toward the sound of her steps on the pavement. His blue eyes locked on her amber eyes, then to her Bolognese dribble, on down to her red Capezio flats, and filled in the rest with his imagination. Just under Fox's two feet, the earth rumbled and squeaked. She looked down at the sauce on her tiny bosom, embarrassed.

ox and Deke were like magnets, or pieces of a puzzle, snapping into place.

From the first day, they could hardly stay away from each other, and though it's fairly impossible to keep a secret on a farm full of snoopy people, they did, and Fox snuck into Deke's bed in the middle of most nights. She knew she had fallen in love, and Deke knew he'd be in big trouble with Jock, Mrs. Jock and both Fox's sisters, if they ever found out he'd de-flowered the youngest member of their family on his very first night on the job.

But, heck, she showed up in his bed that night: just opened the door to the little bunkhouse, padded barefoot across the plank floor, looked at Deke lying on the bunk all splashed with moonlight, pulled her nightgown up and over her head before he could say Jack Rabbit, and slithered buck-naked beside him into the warmth.

He was a goner. He couldn't resist her tender beauty. Her tiny perky breasts spoke his language, and moved him to mur-murings of romantic poetry pouring over her body like a river of love.

Did he love her? He didn't know. He wasn't sure. The Wymans were way above his place—even after his mother's fine home-schooling. He was downright embarrassed by her poverty and despair. Fox (they called her *Fox*—she had some other name on her birth certificate, but no one ever thought of it, and she earned this Fox business, *she noses around like a fox in a hen house*), when she asked him about his family, he lied and said they were from Nova Scotia. He wasn't even sure where Nova Scotia was—it just sounded remote enough that she wouldn't know anything about it. He told her he didn't like to talk about them, anyway, because they were mostly dead, which was true. He didn't tell her that his mother was alive and living in a tin can next to a lapsed Methodist widow and a Choctaw drunk, but he did tell her about the red dust, and the electromagnetic air that burned plants and set the hairs all over your body on end.

He told her about Cimarron County as if it were a bad dream, a moment, a brief time of forgettable proportions, because he couldn't bear to talk about the well or the coughing or the misery or the pain in his mother's eyes as she watched her 11-year-old hack out his final breath and die in her arms. There was nothin' to tell about but death. So, why?

Sweet Farm
Fáno's Soup of Consolation

Jolene hid out in her room for 36 hours. She lay on her side, curled up around *The Hobbit*, the book her grandmother Charlotte had given her as they bolted with minimal luggage from London. The soft yellow bedspread was tucked around her head, leaving just enough natural light for reading. A red finch chirped and eyed her from its place on the bush outside her window.

She knew she was being rude to her cousins but her self-pity overpowered her manners and in a way, she didn't care. They twittered at the door twice, but so far she had gotten away with the "Please No Visitors" sign she wrote with red and black magic markers and taped to her door.

She wasn't trying to be melodramatic. Really.

And besides, they'd probably make fun of *The Hobbit*.

Rita or Fáno or Juana brought her things from time to time: tea, toast, hot water bottle. But the cousins respected the sign.

This was good.

Fáno brought a cup of his "Soup of Consolation"—smooth and creamy, essence of chicken, warm and nourishing, and he would not tell her the ingredients.

"Eet eez a secr-ret, Leetle One. And Eef I tell you, ze magic goez away. Poof! Like dust een ze sky. Eef you drink eet, eet weel make everyone at Zweet Farm happy. You see? Eet eez a cure for them az well az you!"

Jolene was nervous around Fáno at first, but now, she draped the thoughts of perfect father, perfect man around Fáno's shoulders, like a fringed shawl.

Fáno was strong and steady and generous and... well... there. He actually noticed her existence.

And he was so nice to Rita.

And they were so small. Like miniature people, like dolls.

Jolene admitted to herself that there were a few good things about Sweet Farm.

A Job for Nana

I don't know that Chuck is even going to take the job, Noonie. He got up and walked away without a word. I can't make him take it. Maybe you should take it."

"No. No. Absolutely not. He should do it, and I should get a job off-compound. Jim Johnson and his wife are opening a bookstore out in the Village. I heard from Betsy this morning that they're looking for someone to work part time. I'm taking the bus out there to see them tomorrow."

"The bus?"

"The bus. I have no car. And no California license."

"I'll take you, in the truck. I have things I can do out there. I'll go to the hardware store and look at nails, or copper pipes or something."

"Are you sure? You're not going to give me a hard time?"

"Of course I am sure and I won't give you a hard time. I'd rather you stay here and work with us, but I get it. I do. This is a lousy situation. You and the young *Lord* there need some breathing room."

"Right. Yes. Breathing. That would be nice. OK. Good. Help me tell Poppy and Mama, then, please?"

Cousins Keep Trying

 Stevie

By Monday morning, we were at our mutual wits' ends. We were being snubbed!

In the beginning, we gave Jolene the benefit of the doubt. Her period. Check. Her parents. Check. Abruptly yanked out of her surroundings and hauled across the sea. Check. Travel itself! Check that, too.

We weren't her well-mannered, fancy-schmancy British friends. Check and check!

But she'd spent the last 36 hours wallowing in misery in her bed, and we were ready to get on!

Our next tactic in wooing Jolene was to give her a party. In the Hobbit House, of course, where every significant cousin-affecting decision was dissected and the most interesting conversations occurred.

"I know! High Tea! Really! How can she possibly resist?" I said to Tate. She rolled her eyes at me, her usual response to my high flying ideas. She rolled her eyes at her mother with less positive results. "Tate Marie Wyman, I'll give you something to roll about!" Aunt Fox had a short fuse and a sharp sensitivity to foolishness.

But I talked Tate into my latest plan and our preparations began. When we had it just right, on a piece of deckle-edged lavender stationery from Rita's stash in her little built-in desk in the Chapel House kitchen, with my new fountain pen and its purple ink, I hand-wrote an invitation in a combination of cursive and calligraphy hard-learned from Dominicans.

Dear Cousin Jolene,

This is a personal and private invitation to High Tea with your cousins, Tate Wyman and Stevie Michel, in the Hobbit House (ours and yours, only you don't know that yet), in our tree (that you can't see from your window) at 3pm, Monday, August 22, 1960. This is not a fancy affair with long dresses or buttoned up gloves, but a casual party of three. We will have familiar British and French style treats, and you will feel quite at home. We promise readings from Stevie's own writings and musical entertainment by the soon-to-be-famous guitar player and folk singer, Tate "See-Her-Shimmy"* Wyman. For your eyes and ears only.

Remember, 3pm, Today, Come as you are.

We have Rita's "Female Complaint Remedy."

Co-founders of the Girl Cousins' Club at the Hobbit House,

Your dearest and only cousins, Tate & Stevie

*Dear Jolene, I did not write that shimmy part above, Tate

Rita supplied six croissants, lemon curd, strawberry jam, soft butter, sliced salami and ripe cheese, six lavender-lemon zest cookies, two sliced apples, a baguette and a big basket. We put a small bottle of cold milk, sliced lemons, napkins, picnic knives, a checked cloth, three cups with saucers, the basket full of food,  and all the extra items in the little red wagon and hauled it over to the Hobbit. I got up into the tree house and took things from Tate's hands as she handed them up from the wagon.

Tate pushed the red wagon out of the way and swung herself up the ladder and into the Hobbit, just missing the bowl of lemon curd. *Whoa.* If the two of us were having trouble squeezing into the Hobbit, what on earth were we to do with a third person, especially one in tassel loafers, not to mention all the tea things and a guitar? Kicking ourselves for not thinking of this sooner, we considered what to do.

Finally, Tate climbed out and down the ladder and took from me all our careful preparations and put them back into the wagon. We walked over to the Tea Room and borrowed a little table and three chairs, which we hauled out to the Hobbit and sat at the base of the tree—if we couldn't have High Tea *in* the Hobbit, we'd create a Hobbit House veranda.

Misty nosed around the basket. We shooed her away. Tate dashed into the Chapel House to get the flowers while I stayed to protect our investment from menacing and hungry creatures lurking around every tree—dog, cats, birds, Chico. At 10 minutes to 3, I ran into the Tea Room to get the pot of tea from Rita. I covered it with a tea towel, took the handle in my left hand, cupped my right hand around the pot, and, in order not to spill, waddled out to our little party venue under an oak tree.

 Tate

Two days in bed and all that attention while we whispered outside her door like two groveling, sycophantic idiots and she ignored us. I thought she was being a bit over the top. Like her period was that big a deal.

OK. It stung. By rights, as the oldest, I should have been the one to start first. I should've had the first boobs, too, but, ha ha.

I went along with Stevie, but I did not like the way I felt. Brit-envy aside, I was annoyed with this English girl for so many reasons.

 Jolene

I felt better enough to be bored and a bit embarrassed, but hadn't found a graceful way to exit my room—my new cocoon, protection from the vagaries of my parents' relationship. I avoided the inevitable immersion into new life on the compound.

By Monday morning, I regretted my scene on arrival, until I compared it with Nana and Chuck's and realized that the whole mess had been thrust upon me: leaving London in a hurry, for one. And impatient womanhood, not really their fault, but annoying and connected to them anyway. I was on a plane because of their latest botch.

I pulled my resistant self out of the bed about 9 and went into the bathroom to take a hot shower, my first since Saturday morning in the hotel in New York. I washed in lavender soap and put the lavender rinse on my hair. The bathroom did double duty as the laundry room and clean towels were folded on top of the dryer. As I stepped out of the shower I dried myself off and wrapped my head in a towel turban to wick some of the water out of my hair. I put on the white terrycloth robe that hung on the hook on the back of the door and slipped my feet into my fuzzy blue slippers. I stopped at my bedroom door and looked in. I was so busy feeling sorry for myself that I hadn't even noticed my surroundings.

I assessed them now. The room was OK, small, and beige, but Nana said I could paint it. Nice window. The room had been used for storage for a few years, so no bed yet—I was still on the roll-away borrowed from the neighbors. A nice yellow quilt, and a small closet and a dresser. I was going to need a desk and a chair. *A rug would be nice—these terra cotta tiles are cold. But, are we really staying here?*

I got back into the bed, since I was still in shock over the idea that Mama Maria and Poppy had talked Nana into sending me to Santa Lucia School, and I wanted to pull the covers up over my head and think over what was happening to my life. I was secretly wishing they would send me back to London. I could be a boarder at Woolsley, I wouldn't mind at all. I would be away from them. And away from here. Home.

I heard a soft tap. I looked up to see a piece of lavender paper making its way under my closed door, pushed in by two small dusky fingers. The paper quivered once and then was still. I don't know why, but I looked out the window and then, before I looked back to the lavender note, the red finch winked at me. I swear.

I got up and scuffed over to the door, sliding my slippers along the tiles, like snow shoes, shoosh, shoosh, bent down and picked up the piece of paper. As I leaned over, the towel turban slipped off my head. I tossed the towel onto the cot and shook my head to fluff out my wet hair.

On the outside of the folded note was written:

To Jolene Huffington—An Invitation

The lavender note smelled of lavender. Everything smelled of lavender. Lavender ruled the air waves, the ground, the colors of Sweet Farm so deeply that to use any other scent, hue or plant seemed a pity and downright treasonous. I'd only been at Sweet Farm a few days and was overcome already by the penetrating scent. This did not bode well for the rest of my life, considering we'd just blown ourselves onto the farm for, probably, ever.

I opened the folded piece of lavender paper and read my cousins' invitation, written in purple ink. *Geez. Hobbit House? Were they making fun of me? How did they know? And High Tea? Seriously?*

Hobbit House?

I got into the bed, pulled the covers up, and buried my wet head under the pillow. I had to think.

1947

The Denouement

Deke made Fox feel so beautiful. He'd turn her body around and around, using the moonlight if there was any, and his fingers if not, exploring all her nooks and crannies, reveling in her unique narrowness. He said she *looked* like a fox, from head to toe, even the fine hairs on her arms and legs were tinged with red. She was lithe and lean and beasty, he said: she should have been born a four-legged creature.

To Fox, he was just beautiful, naked Deke, there in the night, waiting for her. She loved him. She didn't care a whit about the dust bunnies under the cot or the dishes in the bucket he called his sink.

She had plans: after two years at Monterey Peninsula College (she would be in the first graduating class), she would move to San Francisco and open an art gallery.

"Why San Francisco?" Deke asked one night in the dark.

"Why not?" replied the independent Fox. "San Francisco is a good city, big, no one knows your business."

"Does everyone here know your business?"

"Yes," she said, "they do."

"Not this business," he commented, as he slid his fingers across her mons veneris.

"No, not yet, but they will," Fox said, moving his hand. "Sooner or later they will, and then it won't be the same anymore, because once everyone here knows a secret, well, it's no fun having that secret, because it's not. Do you see?"

"Ye-e-s, kind of. You're telling me you're here with me because it's a clandestine thrill?"

"Well, no, Dekie, I love you," Fox said and paused, looking into his eyes. "But, I want to keep this—you—as mine, just us, and then, when I move on to San Francisco, it will still be mine."

"I see."

Deke couldn't bring himself to ask the obvious question: *Am I in this long range plan of yours?*

But he didn't want to know the answer because, if the answer was yes, then he would have to figure out what to do about it, and if the answer was no, he'd still have to figure out something, because he thought he might love her, and if he did, why, what was he going to do when he had to go to his mother? Say, "C'mon, Fox, come with me to this hell hole in the high desert, where I really grew up, by the way, while I help my mother out of her miserable life in a trailer with a pickled Indian and the Widow Prudence?"

And then, in March, all of that was moot, after Fox uttered those three little life changing words.

August 1960

The Hobbit House, Sweet Farm
Cousins Work It Out

 Tate

Stevie was full of anticipation. Personally, I was uneasy. I think Stevie was onto me, but she kindly didn't say anything.

At 3 o'clock we were ready: our little table covered with the checked cloth, places set, tea paraphernalia all around us—on the ground, on a stool, on a bench from the picnic table.

The blue bachelor buttons were cut short and stuffed into a squat little vase I made in a fourth grade ceramics class—just an over sized pinch pot, but it held water.

By 3:15, Jolene hadn't shown up and I was mad.

Stevie

Tate was all jittery and nervous, I knew she was already irritated by Jolene's little drama, but I had more empathy. Maybe it was Fáno's influence. I knew what it was like to be the odd one out.

I wondered what I would feel like, flying across the sea, being dumped into an unknown land.

By 3:15, though, I was about to make it a committee of two irritated cousins.

Jolene

I stayed buried under the covers reading most of the day, still undecided about going to their little party. Finally, close to 3 o'clock, at the point where Bilbo has just stolen the silver mug from Smaug, the dragon, I got tired of myself and relented. It had to happen sometime. Couldn't put it off any longer. I had to find out what the rest of the family was like.

Besides, I was curious about this Hobbit House business. I put my book down.

I got up and tried to run a brush through my tangled hair. Dried uncombed, it was an eagle's nest—a ponytail would have to do. I sat on the bed, gathered the mop into my left hand and wound a thick hairband around it with my right.

I put on my least citified clothes: navy blue trousers and an over-sized dark green sweatshirt with the Woolsley School emblem on the front and JH embroidered over my heart. The only shoes I had with me were loafers, so... OK, loafers with... no socks. I scrunched my Woolsley cap on over my unruly hair, but when I saw myself in the

bathroom mirror, I looked like a stuffed school mascot, so I let my hair go without the cap or the pony and hoped for the best. I packed a couple of items in my little satchel.

I went back to the rollaway and sat down.

3pm. *Move your buns, Jolene Huffington.*

3:05. Still sitting on the cot. What was I waiting for? *Go!*

3:10. *This is ridiculous. What's the deal? Those girls are waiting for you, be nice!*

I gave myself five more minutes to get it together. I admitted my nervousness to myself: about the girls I hadn't seen in five years; about what a jerk I'd been for two days, acting all Sarah Bernhardt from the moment of arrival; and for my family's shame, agony and tortured relations.

Here they were, Tate and Stevie, leading perfect lives! I was stuck in a bad script.

Finally, 3:15 came and went. I stood up, slung my bag over my shoulder, walked to the door and opened it a crack. I peeked out into the dark and empty hallway. I wondered where my parents were: with luck, somewhere in different quadrants of the universe. I tiptoed down the hall and peeked into the Middle—no one there, either. They were all out and about, doing whatever they did here.

OK.

Go, Jolene.

I tiptoed out into the Middle. I shook my body out, like to get rid of the heebie jeebies, to shed all the attached strings and wires of a puppet and just tried walking like a normal person to the front sliding glass doors.

Looking out, I could see the tree in question, over the gate to the right. It had low-hanging branches, under which there were two pairs of young legs in jeans, seated in little chairs by a table laden with tea paraphernalia.

I pulled my sorry behind out the door and faced my future, who stood up to greet me. Here was tall, elegant Tate, already looking slim and adult (in a sweatshirt just like mine!) and that dark little Stevie, beautiful, spooky grey eyes, long *straight* hair. *I am going to look like a scarecrow next to them.*

 Tate

Finally, her ladyship makes her appearance. Really, I was *this* close to pulling the whole party up into the checked cloth and depositing it in the trash.

Stevie and I exchanged glances. *Check her out,* I thought. Jolene was wearing the duplicate of what I was wearing, except the shoes. And I was in jeans. And she had those amazing breasts. But our oversized sweatshirts with our school emblems and our initials were just the same.

I felt like I was in a slow motion movie, like the wind died down and the birds stopped twittering and a ray of sun shone down on Jolene's red head.

Jolene was so beautiful.

 Stevie

Jolene walked toward us slowly. I think she was really nervous, and I could feel her trepidation vibrate in her step.

It was a pretty mild day for August and we were comfortable in the shade. We already held cups of tea. Rude or not, we waited fifteen minutes for her and we were on the verge of giving up. Well, truth is that Tate was giving-up-ready at two minutes after 3, but I kept saying, "Give her time," and "Hang on," and all kinds of precocious twelve-year-old platitudinous blather. The determined little she-goat in me kept on.

And finally, there she was.

It's funny how certain moments are captured in a frame, while most of the moments in life are gone like dust motes in sunlight, and barely signify. I think there are only a handful of those crystal clear, frameable highlights: falling in love, having a baby, reaching a goal, meeting a true friend, connecting with the Creator.

Here's the freeze frame: Jolene, 5'6" I guessed, full blown woman's body barely concealed by the Tate-look-alike sweatshirt, standing in the afternoon sun in the Adobe House garden, the light striking her hair in that way, that way that made her look on fire.

She gave us a funny, vulnerable sort of grin and walked over to the table.

 Tate

And those shoes!

Excerpt from Stevie's Honors English Journal 1960s Landing in Carmel

For years I thought the name of the hotel by the train station in San Francisco where my grandparents and their daughters stayed the first night was The Little Flea Bag. The Wymans hopped right out of there the next morning and bought a big 1938 burgundy-red Dodge sedan, with a grill in the front of a long hood over a really impressive engine, Poppy said.

They piled their suitcases in the trunk, and the girls and more suitcases in the back seat, and drove to the Monterey Peninsula to look for a likely (meaning big enough) place for their family— with room enough for Jock's books, currently crated in Cleveland. Room also for Maria's studio, her big ideas, boatloads of energy and lots of supplies, bits of furniture to be shipped along soon, three girls, bedrooms for all, enough bathrooms for sanity, and for whatever four-legged creatures they were sure to attract.

They traveled around the Monterey Peninsula, explored the tree-lined streets of Carmel, walked along the Beach, then to the Salinas Valley, explored ranches and roads, back to the Peninsula for three days. They slept one night in the car when they got all turned around out in Carmel Valley near the Arroyo Seco Canyon.

Instead of a house, my grandparents fell in love with a farm, or what was left of an old pear orchard/farmstead, on ten flat, fertile acres at the corner of Schulte and Carmel Valley Roads, in mid Carmel Valley:

> *a dilapidated adobe "main house" with potential for west- and east-end bedroom/bathroom suites and a great-room/kitchen-everything room in the middle;*

> *a funky caretaker's cottage;*

> *a small square building, peak-roofed and spired, known as the Chapel which had been used for a variety of purposes, including sleep, storage and earnest prayers;*

> *a one-story barn on the corner, facing Carmel Valley Road;*

> *all surrounded by big white oaks.*

A dilapidated fixer-upper, if you go by the 1940s black and white photos.

But Maria had a vision and Jock was handy with a hammer. So, they set to work, with an idea that grew all out of proportion in a hurry. Poppy says that before he knew it, "the days flew by and just look what we did. And I wasn't calculating, or throwing up, or frowning anymore."

Chapter Two
Getting to Know You

AUGUST 1960

The Hobbit House
High Tea Part One

Jolene walked over to the little table, eyes on the ground, and squatted to pet the dog, front-paws-all-over-her in a moment... what was her name? *Misty*, she thought. *Nice doggie.*

Misty slobbered on Jolene and then jumped down, sniffed at the table and toddled off to lie in a patch of shade.

The two other girls waited, awkward but resolute. Jolene stood up, dusted the Misty debris off her pants and put out her hand. Her face was concealed by her hair, a technique reserved for those occasions when there was nothing else behind which to hide.

First Stevie and then Tate took Jolene's hand. It was quiet for a moment, while they looked at those three hands, held together by an invisible string. Stevie and Tate looked up at each other and to the top of Jolene's red head. Jolene blew her hair out of her face and looked up into their eyes, one to the other.

Misty kept her eye on the table.

1947

Consequences

Deke was worried. Seven months on this job and dang it, he was beginning to like it too much. What with Fox n' all, and the Wymans, why, a guy could settle down.

But, Ma... I have to get back to help Ma. She doesn't even know where I am.

If I save enough, I can get her outta there in a coupla months, and we can go somewhere so she can have some peace and quiet.

I got $1300 saved so far, wrapped in a sock under my cot. Just a bit more and I can go for her...

I could never bring Ma here, could never get that close. I'd have to tell them the truth. And tell her the truth! Ma doesn't even know where I am!

But Fox... man, I sure as all get-out love bein' with her. All that jumpin' around in the bed in the middle of the night. And she can talk about stuff, and she's funny.

"I am pregnant." Fox said those three little words in the quiet, lovely, sexy warm afterglow of their night. It came out light, like, "Let's have pancakes." But it wasn't.

Deke's naked right arm curled around her and wispy orange Fox hair tickled his chest. The cigarette in his left hand burned down to a long, curving ash before he croaked out a response. This definitely was not funny.

"What?"

"I said, I am pregnant." She looked at him with those smoldering, hot amber-gold eyes, as if she weren't 17; as if he weren't an itinerant worker from No Man's Land; as if Jock, the best boss he'd ever had, was not going to kill him with his bare hands when he found out.

"Wh... ugh, how much pregnant?"

"There are no degrees of pregnant, Dekie. I am wholly, absolutely, 100% pregnant. I am going to have a baby. Your baby. In September."

"Dang," he said.

"Thanks," she said. "That makes me feel really good."

"Well, what'll you do?" he asked, not knowing what the heck else to say, stumbling over every stupid word out of his flipping mouth.

"*What will I do?*" she asked. "Are you serious? Isn't it more, '*What will WE do?*' Did I make this baby alone, Deke?"

"Well, no, honey, no, but, well, I wasn't plannin' on having a kid this minute. I mean, I gotta do this *thing*, and...I..."

"Well, it looks to me like the next *thing* you gotta do is stand by me while I tell my parents. I don't want you to marry me, Deke. I don't want to get married. My precautions just stopped working. I've thought about this, so please, hear me out here, before you flip all out and get crazy on me, before you tell me your life just stopped in its tracks, because that is how I feel, and one of us is enough right this minute. I'll have this baby. You'll stay with me, at least til she's grown enough so I can go back to school, and then you can go if you want. But, please, don't make me do this alone, or face my parents alone. My sisters will come home eventually from their post-war adventures, but I am on the spot here at the farm without them right now, our parents' focus is all on me, and I have to figure this all out before I tell them. Please tell me you'll stay."

Deke, still in shock, his puzzle pieces suddenly all up in the air and raining down on his head, was not a swearing man, but he pondered some good sparkly ones while he was working out what to say to this beautiful, complex pregnant creature beside him.

An Excerpt from Stevie's Honors English Journal 1960s
The Farm

20 yeas ago, this Farm was somebody's dashed dream. I never met the former owners, the Macintoshes, but I hear they lost their shirts in the Depression and never got back on their feet. Or something.

When Jock and Maria moved into the caretaker's cottage (to give the Macintoshes time to move out of the Adobe), the barn was leaning slightly south and the cottage leaked in about 100 places. They patched the leaks, painted the tiny cottage and moved a series of caretakers in and out until the Rodriguezes came along and stayed, before I was born. Chico is their only child, a "late in life" baby, born au natural in their cottage. They basically treat him like a god. He's 3.

My grandparents did most of the work themselves—it became my grandfather's "little tranquilizer," he said. "I could see right off that your grandmother had a plan, Stevie, and, well, I figured she got us here in one piece, or five pieces, and I was, well, I was just tired of the fight—not with her, but with IT, with my life, with working against my nature. It's like walking into a 60 mile an hour wind. It's hard work, and beats on your head. Particularly if you're in denial. So I surrendered. I could do nothing but! And then I started bangin' nails and swingin' a hammer, and fixing things and, well, it felt just fine. And John Steinbeck? Why, maybe I'll meet him someday."

Since 1940, when they purchased Sweet Farm, Poppy's been to all Mr. Steinbeck's favored spots, many times each. In 1945, he read the newly published Cannery Row *while sitting on a bench on Cannery Row, at that time still known as Ocean View Blvd. He read it once and then read it through again, right away. He stood outside Doc Ricketts' lab and stared in the windows for long minutes, imagining the parties and the smell of fishes and octopi and beer and fancy girls and fried meat. Beginning in 1959, he slipped through the beaded curtain at Kalisa's La Ida Cafe, where, in John Steinbeck's world, Wide Ida ruled and Eddie the bartender poured all the leftover drinks into a jug for the boys. He sat at a certain round green table and sipped black coffee, idling away a few hours each week contemplating the ghosts of Cannery Row's hottest ladies of the evening. He smelled Dora's perfume, heard the rustle of her skirts, the rasp of her voice.*

"Which came first? my grandfather would ask, "Cannery Row or *Cannery Row?*"

"The book came first! And the name of the street was officially changed in 1958 in honor of it!"

Sometime in the 50s, Mr. Steinbeck moved to New York, so the chances of their meeting grow slimmer.

 Tate

When Jolene looked about to bolt, Stevie was the first to speak. Stevie has ever been the first to do anything, except her menses.

She said, "Please sit down," and gestured to the seat in the middle facing the Adobe, in which Jolene dutifully sat.

"We have an announcement, which I wrote down. Please bear with me while I get it together. Hghmph...

"Proclamation: To Jolene Huffington, only other cousin of the Wyman Clan, we offer you one third membership of the tribe known as The Girl Cousins' Club and one third ownership of the clubhouse, known as the Hobbit House. No Boys Allowed. It is only for us.

"Further, let it be known that Mr. Stefáno Michel, Fáno, my dad, has committed to helping the club members THIS WEEK, which means, in one of his native languages, 'really soon.' We will add a few feet onto the platform of the Hobbit House and construct a new house to accommodate its latest and, as far as we know, last member, since we are old and our mothers aren't likely to have any more girls.

"We officially welcome you to Sweet Farm, but even more officially, into The Girl Cousins' Club. And the Hobbit."

Me? I sat there picking at my cuticles, thinking how brilliant was my cousin Stevie.

An Excerpt from Stevie's Honors English Journal 1960s

TEA

Tea is an aromatic and often caffeinated beverage, served hot or cold, prepared by pouring boiled water over the cured dried leaves of Camellia sinensis, *the tea plant, or other herbs. After four or five minutes steeping, you've got tea. Pour it in a cup.*

Earliest noted tea drinkers were the 10th-century Chinese. Phonetically, in Chinese, it is pronounced cha or, *from the* Persians, chai. *In French,* thé.

Japanese and Chinese tea ceremonies are filled with ritual and meaning. High Tea *is a tradition in England, with sweet as well as savory items, often substantial enough to replace supper. French tea rooms are filled with confections and tea and coffee. In Thailand, tea is served cold with sweetened condensed milk.*

In our house, we believe that tea is medicine, just like any herb. It is revered.

Black tea is for energetic focus.

Green tea is for calm focus.

Lavender and mint for relaxation.

Chamomile for sleep.

The Camellia sinensis *likes lots of rain, acidic oil and high elevations, so they will grow slowly and gain more flavor.*

Harvested tea leaves must be dried carefully and quickly to avoid mold or bacteria, which would render the tea useless.

Teas can be blended, sold in bags, and have additions such as orange peel or dried pomegranate.

At the Sweet Tea Room, there are 20 kinds of black and green teas from around the world: China, Formosa, Japan, India.

Herbal teas, such as chamomile, lavender, mint, St. John's wort, etc., come from the Sweet Farm garden. Lemon, orange, and valerian, too.

Tea is said to be the second most consumed beverage on Earth, after water.

80% of the tea consumed in America is iced tea.

 Jolene

There was so much I didn't understand.

Then, Stevie finally stopped talking, saw my blank face and pointed behind me. I turned around to see what I had not noticed before, so focused was I on my feet and the ground.

There it was. The Hobbit House. It looked built by beavers. Or squirrels. The walls were old warped slats and logs, with knots and little branches sticking out, all spaces filled with moss and leaves.

And the roof! It was practically all moss: an off-center, softly peeked construction, held down by some chicken wire. Handmade arrows and little stick people and charms were stuffed into the moss—buttons and spoons, acorns and shells, strings of beads.

The windows looked like they'd been cut with a pocket knife, all funky, with slashes, no straight lines. There were three little boards nailed to the tree that served as a ladder. I could barely see inside—redwood deck, a piece of carpet, sun shining in mottled pools on the floor.

I held my breath.

 Tate

This is my part, so I'll talk next. We decided that with your coming to Sweet Farm, it is time for an initiation to happen. No, don't look like that, It does not involve anything stupid or scary. Well, maybe it's scary. Stevie and I have lived here all our lives, so it is all natural to us—this tree, the club, the tree house. The Hobbit House was built four and a half years ago, right after your last visit. But, in fairness, we want to start out with you equally, since you're here and all. Sorry, that didn't sound very nice, and I didn't mean it that way. Oh, this is coming out all wrong!

"See, we are three now. So, to be equal, we are going to have a moment of Truth with a capital T. Not today, because we are each going to think about our truth and tell the capital T Truth on the day that the new improved Hobbit House is completed and we are sitting in it, three together. Believe me, until then, we won't fit.

"Our Truth Story is a sort of blood mingling, without the razor. Although as cousins, we are already blood related. But this is a... a... what was it, Stevie? Oh yeah, a metaphor. It is the story of us, ugly and beautiful, including our biggest fear and our craziest hope. It is the real us, safe forever among us three. See, everything in the tree house belongs to us. Including secrets, so, whether you write it down or just tell the story, the Hobbit House is, like, the safest place you'll ever be."

 # Stevie

"So," I said. "Would you like some tea?"

An Excerpt from Stevie's Honors English Journal 1960s
Lavandula

When they moved to the farm, my grandmother was in possession of some premium Lavandula angustifolia seeds, sent from her cousin André, the herb farmer in France. It takes hundreds of tiny seeds to get just a few plants—better to buy seedlings, she says. But, once they get started, well, there is no stopping lavender plants. Maria planted 10,000 lavender seeds in little trays and watered them every day and spoke to them in French, sang to them in their native lavender tongue, whatever that is, lavender-ese, and even, Poppy says, "hummed to them in Spanish."

She said she grew enough seedlings to set out a few rows per year for five years, and then she stopped seeding—it had come time to divide up the older plants—she said it was like keeping up with multiplying rabbits.

"That all sucked up the acreage pretty quick," Poppy said, "and soon we were living on a lavender planet."

As her three girls were growing up, going to high school, college (one and a half of them), getting married (two of them), Maria and Poppy built this little farmette, a family compound, with the help of Felix and Juana Rodriguez.

The Sweet Farm barn is Douglas fir, stained the color of tea. The front of the barn faces toward Carmel Valley Road, with a ferny, north-side garden, full of Cineraria and mint, calla lilies and Hosta.

Lavandula is the center of gravity at Sweet Farm. The upper half of Lavandula's dutch door is always open, pressed all the way around right to the wall, and closed only if it's windy.

When you enter Lavandula, you wonder how it ever was a barn. It is full of color and crafts and supplies for crafts—a feast for artists' eyes.

Customers bury their hands in baskets of yarn and run their fingers across velvety fabric stacks. The pungent smells of water colors and glue, fabric, old paper and wood chips blend with herbs and garden and lavender soap. The lavender-washed walls catch the sunlight.

Maria makes essential oils, candles, sachéts, pillows, herb blends, wreaths and soap from her lavender harvest.

In the center of the big open space is a table—really an antique 6' x 8' barn door polished to the smoothness of a baby's patooty, varnished and sanded and varnished 6 times, and placed on two stumps of redwood. It's an awesome workbench—women sit there in these comfy stool-chair-thingies that Poppy designed— they quilt and knit and make candles, come in and out, get up and down, bees buzzing, chatter pattering, consuming bazillions of cups of tea...

Which brings me back to Rita and Fáno coming home from France in 1948 with some new plans.

Well, it was coming home for her, only with a surprise husband and the surprise—the growing tummy-ful of me!

For Fáno, it was... a whole different kettle of fish. I know he was a 28 year old, 5'1" 100-pound half-French orphan, whose "home" was a fractured France, and no longer his home at all. I know he had minimal English and was in love with a beautiful little American nurses' aid. That's what I know.

High tea continues, still...

Jolene

Stevie poured tea for me from a small porcelain pot into a thin tea cup with mismatched saucer.

There were all kinds of good things to eat, but, for the moment, I was mesmerized by my cousins.

What a goofball you are, Jolene Huffington. You've missed out on two days of Tate and Stevie by holing yourself up in your room under the covers.

Stevie was prattling on about something to do with Uncle Fáno collecting new/old wood for the Hobbit House and Tate was busy fiddling with the tea things. I was awkward, not knowing what to do or say, except my ongoing inner commentary.

"And then," Stevie went on, "we are going to take down the walls and put up the boards from the Simpson's warehouse and..."

"Could I see it?" I finally ventured.

Tate looked up and Stevie looked up and their words collided into one, "What?"

"The Hobbit House. Can I see inside?"

"Ha! Oh, sure!" said Stevie as she got up, dusting croissant crumbs off her lap. "Silly us! It's the most important thing! C'mon."

Which was where we'd left off the other night.

We couldn't, indeed, all fit into the Hobbit House, so they let me go in by myself. I climbed up the little ladder, slipping in my loafers—*these shoes will have to go,* I thought.

I crawled into the tiny room, and found myself in another world. There were pillows and blankies and a soft piece of carpet to sit on; drawings of hobbits and gnomes and elvish-looking creatures were haphazardly tacked up to the dusty gold walls. The yellow checked curtains fluttered in the easterly breeze. All around the walls near the mossy ceiling were tacked gold and silver Christmas tree garlands, draped and looped in and around themselves. Painted on the walls were some kind of symbols, runes or elvish, I didn't know. I could see the roof was water tight—it had been made by a pro, someone who had obviously done this before.

Tate and Stevie poked their heads in the door.

"Do you like it?" one of them asked.

I started to cry.

 # Tate

Oh, no. *Now what? I thought. Am I truly going to be sorry I have this other cousin?*

 # Stevie

Jolene started to cry. I wasn't sure why, but I wasn't going to let it get in the way of this new feeling I had—that something special was happening.

"What is it, Jo?" I asked.

She snuffled and wiped her nose on the paper napkin Tate handed to her. When she had regained composure, she whispered, "I am so sorry."

"For what?" we both asked.

"For being such a monumental moron. It's just that everything is so messed up, so crazy, so..."

"Yeah. We know. And, hey, don't think we don't have things that are screwed up, too. We've all got a story."

"Can't be as bad as mine."

"Well," I said. "Maybe not right this minute. But, wait until our Truth Party. It'll all come out."

We were quiet for a moment. Jolene unfolded her legs, climbed back down the ladder and sat with us at the table. Tate went into the Tea Room with the pot to get a refill. Jolene sliced open a croissant and filled it with Lemon Curd.

"Did Aunt Rita make this?" she asked with her mouth full.

"Yeah. She makes everything. She's a little powerhouse baker, never stops moving; my mother is like a wind-up toy."

"It's delicious. Just like home. Er, you know."

"I know." I didn't, but I could guess she was homesick.

When Tate returned, she poured more tea and sat down.

Jolene reached into her satchel and pulled out a book covered with stiff brown paper, like the shopping bags we turned inside out to cover our school books.

Handing it to me, she said, "Can we talk about this?"

I opened it. I suppressed a smile and showed it to Tate.

The look on Tate's face was worth the whole long drawn out business of getting to know Jolene. She was finally grinning. And, for once, not rolling her eyes.

"*The Hobbit!*"

# An Excerpt from Stevie's Honors English Journal 1960s Fáno & Rita

Fáno could cook. Fáno could garden. Fáno could sew a straight line! Fáno could swing a hammer and that went a long way with Poppy.

Did I say it took three months for Mama Maria to accept Fáno? She told me in her interview for my journal that she knew right away, as soon as Rita and Fáno were in the Adobe House kitchen together, that she had misjudged him, but it took her three months to admit it. They were so beautiful together, she said, small and compact—they fit like old shoes.

She gave him the cold shoulder from pride, but grinned inside at his antics, his mysticism, his difference. He eventually won her heart.

Personally, I think it was the sewing.

He took over the distillery, too, and made essences of other things besides lavender—orange and mint and sage.

One day, Rita went to her mother with a proposal. She had nothing to do at Sweet Farm—every job was filled. Nana was in London doing whatever she did there; Deke managed the fields; Fox was at the college and nursing Tate between classes; Maria did the bookkeeping, Poppy was... just Poppy. Even Fáno was fitting in.

"Where am I in all this?" Rita asked. "I need meaning. I need a project. I want to open a tea room. Over there," she pointed *through the east wall in Lavandula.* "In the unfinished front section of the barn, your storage. We'll call it the Sweet Tea Room. We have a built-in clientele: your ladies who come to craft and sew with you, for starters. For years now you've had a kettle on for tea."

Her mother, who had been bending over the workbench pinning squares together for a dark green and blue patchwork quilt she called the Forest Floor, peered at her daughter over half-glasses.

Her art-pal, Davina, painted a Carmel Comstock House mailbox: curving shingle roof line, rounded doors, a little bungalow for fairies, dolls and mail. Her eyes didn't leave her brush, but her ears were pinned to the conversation. She was, for certain, enjoying a cup of English breakfast tea with lemon and honey. And a biscuit.

"A tea room?" said Rita's mother.

"Yes."

"You weesh to charge people now for something they have had as a natural part of their experience at Lavandula for eight years?"

"Yes."

"Do you think they will pay for thees?"

"Yes, because it will be different. Delicious. Scones and lemon curd and tea cookies and little savory bits. Then, later we can add soups or salads, bread and then we can do a special High Tea between 2 and 5 and..."

"Wait, ma chérie, give me a moment, my darling."

"I've thought it through, Mama, and here it is, on paper. I've worked it all out for opening 4 days a week at first, then if it goes, six, with Sundays always closed, and we can be open from 11-5, and I've talked to Fox and she thinks we can do it and Poppy says it's alright with him. Of course, I'd have to borrow the money from you."

Maria, who hadn't moved, gazed at her daughter's protruding tummy, due to expel its little passenger any minute. Rita looked down. Davina looked up.

"Mmm. Well, we'll all do it, then," said the ever-enthusiastic Rita. "We'd all have to pitch in, anyway. Will you be my partner, Mama? Please? It'll be fun!"

"I am sure it will be fun, ma chérie, but will it make money? I am not happy to lose money, you know."

"It will make money, Mama. I know it."

1947

Sweet Farm
A Slight Change of Plans

Jock paced twelve steps: east/west, west/east, wearing a path in the carpet in his little study. His face showed all the emotions he could not yet verbally express: hurt, betrayal, sorrow, fear for his youngest daughter.

Fox was cornered, with her imaginary fluffy red tail between her legs, which were quivering, but she held her ground.

Deke, on the other hand, sat in the bunkhouse waiting for news. She called him a coward. He called it survival. "I need my neck to stay on my shoulders, darlin," he said.

"How long has this been going on?" asked Jock.

"Since last summer."

"Last summer? Last summer? I must not be hearing you right."

"You're hearing me right, Poppy. I love Deke."

"You're 17, Fox."

"Almost 18."

"Have you told your mother?"

"No. Just you. And Deke."

"Oh, ho! And what did Deke Harley have to say for himself?"

"Not much, really. He's... he's afraid you'll strangle him. That you'll think it's his fault."

"Isn't it? He's 23, Fox. He's supposed to be an adult. I trusted him, thought he was an OK guy, even though he's a drifter and all he owns is a pretty blue bike. Now this... I might just strangle him."

"He's more than an OK guy, Poppy. He loves me, too. I don't think he knows it yet, but he does. And, if it's anyone's fault, it's mine."

"And just how is that?"

"Well, he didn't have much of a chance. I showed up in the night and..."

"What night?"

"Oh, er, uhm... his first night."

This was hard to take. Jock swallowed his first remark, which had something to do with her slutty behavior with a total stranger, but it was too late for that. He couldn't deny that he had seen sparks fly between the two on Deke's arrival. And since.

But, of his three girls, Fox had shown the most promise. She wasn't dramatic, like Nana, or dreamy, like Rita. Just driven. And, generally, pragmatic.

He did wonder what was tempering her these last few months. Now he knew: hot sex in the night with a handsome Nova Scotian. He shook his head to get the picture out of his mind.

"And since you seem to have figured this all out, what are your next moves? What does this do to your future planning? I don't see a baby on your hip in a San Francisco Gallery..."

"I won't marry him, if that's what you're getting at. I don't want to get married, and neither does he. But he'll stay. And we'll have this baby together. And then we'll see."

"Your mother will be disappointed in you, Fox. You have the most potential. You have no idea how a baby will change your life. A baby is forever. You will be asking a lot of your family, to take in a sneaking liar, who, in retrospect, has shown me for the fool. Every day he was eating our food, taking his paycheck, smiling all the while, and coupling with my youngest daughter by night."

"Poppy...."

"Am I wrong? Put yourself in my place and see the picture wholly for a moment. You're under-age. I could have him arrested for statutory rape. It doesn't matter that you started it. He's older and is supposed to have a better grip... Well, he's supposed to know better."

There was, shall we say, a pregnant five minute pause while each of the Wymans present considered his or her thoughts. Jock stopped pacing and looked out the window. His coffee was as cold as a Colorado morning and it was too early for this conversation. Maria was already in Lavandula, getting ready for a class. He would have to wait until evening to tell her.

And he would have to see Deke. Now.

Fox sat very still in her chair, tail twitching, watching her father while he hoisted her problem onto his shoulders. *This is not the end of the world*, she thought. *Just a set back. Just a baby. Dekie's baby.*

"Are you prepared for the social stigma, Fox? An unwed mother? Do you propose to live with Deke here?"

"I don't care what people think, Poppy. Yes, we'll be here, if you'll have us. You can tell the whole world we are married, if you want, but I am not going to marry him. I just don't feel like I should ever get married. I don't know why. But this baby, she needs to be born. And she needs to know her father. I don't know what will happen, but Deke has committed to staying here for now, and that is all I can ask. All I want."

"You're sure it's a girl?"

"I am sure of everything."

He knew that was bravado, but he did not argue the point.

Deke sat on the bench outside the bunkhouse, whittling a stick. It was just a stick. He didn't whittle or express anything in particular: no protective symbols, like Fáno. Slicing slivers off the small piece of soft pine was enough action to keep him from jumping out of his skin. It's all he could ask.

It was a warm March day, and the sun against the south wall of the bunkhouse helped sooth his jagged nerves.

Jock came around the corner with frosty bottles of lemonade from the Tea Room. Deke appreciated the gesture, but was not fooled. *There will be hell to pay here, I know. I deserve it.*

Jock said, "Too early for alcohol. Cold Duck would certainly be more appropriate."

The family joke was lost on Deke, who looked away. Jock handed him a bottle and sat down on the bench right up close, making Deke very uncomfortable, indeed.

And worse? Jock did not utter a word for the longest ten minutes of Deke's life.

Finally, looking straight out to Saddle Mountain, focusing on the tree tops, gripping the bottle and wondering if the young man beside him was trying to decide whether to surrender or bolt, Jock said, "She's under-age for this, boy."

"Yes sir, I know."

"Do you take responsibility? Are you in it for the long haul? If you hurt her, or leave her, I'll come after you. I will."

1949

Sweet Farm
Deke & the Kid

Deke lay on the grass with his head on a pillow snatched from the sofa on his way out the door. Nestled in the crook of his arm was his little daughter, Tate, wrapped up tight in a soft blue blanket. It was midnight, and they were both awake, pondering the stars. Deke pointed out the Milky Way to his perky little pal.

Tate liked to slip over the crib railing and toddle into Deke and Fox's room in the barn apartment to roust Deke out of bed. She'd poke his nose gently with her pointer finger, and whisper, "DeDe–me!" and laugh when he opened his eyes. He'd reach a hand out from under the covers and she'd latch onto his fingers and tug until he got up. Her need wasn't hunger, so he could let Fox sleep. He picked the little one up and tiptoed out the door. The two-year-old Tate had discovered the night.

Deke pointed out the Big Dipper in the north. He had no idea if she knew, at 2, what the heck he was talking about, but he talked just the same, thinking the sound of his voice was all that mattered.

This night, she hummed. He was telling her about the North Star, and she started humming. He'd stop, she'd stop, he'd start, she'd start, and so on and on. She laughed and laughed. Her first joke. And the first of many hums. Tate was no talker, but there were sound effects aplenty wherever she went. Tate's first musical instrument was her grandmother's upside-down soup pot on which she joyfully whacked with a big wooden spoon. When the pot became too dented to perform its job on the stove without wobbling, Maria surrendered it to the toy box.

Cousin Stevie's interests, at 1, were eating, sleeping and playing patty-cake, but she liked to lie on her blanket and listen to Tate make a gleeful racket with the pots and pans. She patty-caked in devoted appreciation: Tate's built-in audience of one.

Tate snuggled right into the comfort of her father's arms on their nighttime visits to the cosmos. He smelled like new shoes and honey. She didn't have a clear picture of the subject matter he prattled on about, or the specifics of the starry night, or what exactly was a constellation, but her gaze never left the view of the dark and glittery expanse above them. The midnight sky floated like a blanket of soft sounds to her, a comforter filled not with feathers but music. She could stay there all night, happily sleeping in her father's arms under moonlight and star songs, and she balked when Deke rose after an hour to return to their respective beds. But they hummed their way to her little room, and by the time they arrived at her pillows, she was snoring softly into his armpit. Deke knew his daughter. He tucked her in and touched her fine blonde hair with his rough hand. A splash of moonlight lit her face. He paused for a moment, looking at his sleeping little girl-child.

When he slipped back into his bed, Deke wrapped his lanky self around Fox's warm lithe body. She murmured, half awake, half dreaming, "Did you wake the moon?"

The Middle, Sweet Farm
Chuck Doesn't Play the Piano

Chuck sat at the baby grand piano in the middle of the Middle and wrote a poem that had been buzzing in his head for days. His cigarette lay burning in the groove in the ashtray, long grey ash curving and about to drop.

My world is on fire

She sang to the choir

These days are all jumbled and torn

My life is mess

Just look at my dress

I am shamed, disregarded and scorned

Please give me some rest

I have failed this test

I am weary and want to lie down

I have loved and I've lost

But my stars are still crossed

And I'll never wear the gold crown

Oh when will this stop and

When will I drop

All this pretense and fooling around

My life is near done

I've lost and they've won

And I lie with my face to the ground

Well, how cheery, he thought.

Chuck shook the ash from his Benson & Hedges and took a long drag. Blowing out the smoke in a wobbly ring, he studied the piano keys in front of him. The keys looked foreign to him, dead. White white black white black white. So what?

He crushed out the fag and took a sip from his drink. It was four in the afternoon, and Chuck was tired.

Jock slid open the glass front door and stepped into the room carrying a load of firewood in a canvas sling. He set the sling on the floor in front of the fireplace and stacked the wood to the right. He glanced at Chuck, who did not notice.

Jock went back out to the wood stack, collected another load, carried it into his and Maria's room through the other sliding glass door, setting the wood to the right of the fireplace.

He walked back into the living room and said to Chuck, "Mind if I join you?"

Chuck looked up, startled out of a dark revery. "Oh! Uhm. Yes. Sure. Jock. I was just, ah, sitting here."

"I'll pour myself a drink. Top yours off?"

"No. No. I'm good. I'm... thanks."

Jock, who had been sent by Maria and Fox to take Chuck's pulse, set the canvas sling by the door and walked over to the bar. He took his time, clinking ice, pouring, wiping the bottle, putting things away.

He sat down in the chair nearest the piano, facing Chuck.

"What's that you're writing?"

"Nothing."

"Nothing?"

"Nothing, Jock. Just scribbles."

"Ah."

Jock was at a loss. His mission was clear, but the women hadn't provided a script, and he was no shrink.

"Chuck..." he began. "We should... ah, talk about some things."

"Oh?"

"Mmm... Yes. You know, it's been almost a week now, and you and I haven't really had a conversation, so..."

"I haven't felt much like talking."

"Be that as it may, Chuck, we still need to clarify what's to be done."

"Done?"

"Well, how we are to proceed. I understand you've given Fox no real answer, and she is hoping you'll join her in the work here. Nana has her job in the Village and..."

Chuck's eyes flared. "She what? What job? She didn't tell me."

"Have you talked to her, Chuck? It would behoove you to communicate with your wife."

"Please, Jock. Don't lecture me. I know what I should be doing."

"I am not lecturing, and I did not say *should*." Jock warmed to his subject. "I said it would be a good idea. Now, you've come here, and we are happy to have you, but we need help, and I find it right odd you haven't figured out that you have arrived in time to save us, yes, save us, from a current crisis of staffus-interruptus. See, we saved you—you can return the favor."

"Well, that's blunt."

"My style, my boy. Get it out there. Everyone will be better for it. I learned that the hard way."

"What's this about Nana? A job." Chuck fidgeted on the piano bench, swirling the ice in his glass, lighting another Benson & Hedges with the one about to burn his fingers. His ears were red, from anger or shame? We'll never know.

"She'll be working part time in the new bookstore in the Village, The Dream Catcher. I am sorry to be the one to tell you your wife's business, but, there you are."

"Why isn't she working here, at Sweet Farm?"

"Because she thought she should leave that to you. Perhaps she thought the air would do you good. Something different. And, she knows books. She'll be happy there."

"Hghmph."

Jock ignored this and said, "So, what's it to be, Chuck? Let's be frank. We've paid your way here, we have opened up our home, we have agreed to send Jolene to Santa Lucia, so..."

"What? You're kidding, right? What? You've decided where my child will go to school? Do I not have a say in this?"

"Well, I imagine that if you were speaking to Nana, you would have been in the conversation. As it is, we never know where you are, and you do not contribute your thoughts, so we roll along, making decisions..."

"Hah. And taking over my life."

"You're bitter, Chuck. With no reason. At least not toward us. We are definitely not taking over your life. We are taking care of our family. We are offering you a job, a way to contribute to the care of our family—and I use the term expansively—*our family*. We are all in this together, son-in-law and, good or bad, you're pretty much stuck here, so I'd say deal with it."

Later, he couldn't say where this came from, but the next words out of his mouth were decisive.

"But, bottom line is, I give you 24 hours to show up in the office and offer your services to Fox, or, well, get out. One or the other. It's time."

"It's been barely a week!" Chuck squeaked.

"It's been 14 years, Chuck, my friend. Do you know the definition of insanity?"

"Yes... No."

"It's when you cannot distinguish fantasy from reality. Join the family reality or get on."

The Super Conductor was nowhere in sight.

Chuck's Confession

Chuck choked on his gin. He got so, so quiet. In his heart, he knew Jock was right. Chuck was PO'd at the world, like Nana, but he *knew* how much of the whole mess had been his fault. And maybe he *was* insane. Or possessed.

He looked at his father-in-law and whispered, "OK."

Some quiet moments went by. Jock sat in the chair, musing. Chuck rose from the piano and wandered around the room, touching things: the red stained glass lampshade on the bar; the little heart rock on the windowsill; a shell from a Carmel Beach picnic; a petrified acorn from the Arroyo Seco Gorge; a little pewter spoon from Williamsburg, Virginia.

"It is all my fault, you know."

"What is?"

"Coming here. Being broke. Being chucked. Ha ha. I just thought of that. Chucked. We've been Chucked. Splendid."

"What happened?"

What happened, indeed, Chuck thought.

Chuck had been so sure he was going to make it this time. He didn't realize that he'd drained the accounts; hadn't expected Guy Whatsit to abscond, to dump him like a box of baked rocks; he hadn't known they were *this* close to the edge. He thought he was *saving* Jolene's future.

And now this last—the bills were enormous, the apartment gone, the life transformed in an instant. No, not an instant—Jock was right, it's taken years to go sour, one step after another down the slippery slope.

I can't seem to help it, he thought. *An old wolf haunts me.*

Chuck was so quiet that Jock thought he might not answer, but when he did... when he did, there was so much sorrow in his simple response, such a broken sound, it made Jock weep.

"I believed a lie."

 Tate

Yes, I was 2½ at the time. But I missed my dad when I didn't see him anymore. For a long while I heard excuses regarding his whereabouts: he was cutting hay in Idaho; gone to pick up a new truck; met some old friends at the rodeo. After a while, my folks on Sweet Farm gave up the fantasy of his ever coming back, and, when I asked about DeDe, they said, "He's gone."

I missed the spicy aroma of leather and bees that lingered in his wake. And I missed our nights. My mother wasn't the least bit interested in continuing any nocturnal excursions and, when I'd come to her room for midnight companionship, she put me firmly back in my bed.

"This cannot become a regular thing, Tatie, and I am not going to get up in the middle of the night. Go to sleep, like a normal person. Please. Just one night. All night. Please."

She didn't get it. I was awake! At midnight. Fortunately, I soon discovered that Stevie was up for any adventure, day or night. We often slept in each other's rooms, or in the garden in sleeping bags, and later, of course, in the Hobbit.

In a frenetic fit my mother got rid of all the pictures of my father so I forgot what DeDe looked like and eventually I forgot the nickname. I heard them talking about Deke's blue bike once, but I remembered only his aftershave and the Big Dipper and that he left us and that his name was Deke.

My loss was my mother. She cried alone. I knew I was missing a major piece of a puzzle, and I couldn't find it in her anywhere, and I was crying, but I didn't know exactly why. She never found solace in me, either. She took over Deke's job at Sweet Farm and fobbed me off on Juana and Mama Maria and Aunt Rita. I'm not bitter, but facts are facts. We slept in the same house, but that was all. The pain got too big to share.

When he dropped out of sight, Fox defined herself as *the Woman Deke Left*. She made a lot of assumptions on the way to that definition.

An Excerpt from Stevie's Honors English Journal 1960s
Lavandula angustifolia

Angustifolia *is the Latin word for "narrow leaved." Flower stems of* Lavandula angustifolia *are unbranched, with a single flower head on each straight stem. All varieties have a sweet fragrance. Flower colors range from deep purple to white.*

The folklore of lavender dates back to the Romans, when the women picked wild lavender off the coastal rocks to scent their baths and sooth their brows. The Romans brought it with them when they conquered England in about 43AD.

Throughout the Middle Ages, European monasteries cultivated lavender and other herbs in the "physick gardens" used for concoctions and remedies. The famous nun, Hildegard of Bingen, created a cure for migraines using lavender with vodka or brandy in the 11th century.

Lavender has been considered effective against everything from apoplexy and loss of speech to restlessness and insomnia. It's used as protection from the evil eye as well as a cure for bites from venomous snakes and mad dogs.

It takes about 500 pounds of flowers to produce 1½ pounds of essential oil. It is mostly from the Mediterranean, and grows where summers are long, winters are mild, and the humidity is low, like Carmel Valley. Lavender likes well-drained soil, but grows on rocks and sprouts between bricks. It likes nitrogen.

Lavender is drought tolerant, but it needs regular watering to produce flowers for harvest (rather than just a hedge or driveway trim or whatever).

My grandmother started her acres of lavender from 10,000 seeds, but she guesses only about 100 seedlings actually made it into the ground. She started propagating by cuttings and separating plants right away, which she says is the way to go. She has around 2500 plants per acre, and about six of our ten acres are in lavender, so that means there are about 15,000 plants out there. I've never counted. Fáno says he's gotten close, but he either loses count about half way through or something interrupts him, mostly Rita. Or someone plants more.

As it nears harvest time, Mama Maria and Rita like to drape sheets and towels to dry over the lavender plants to absorb the fragrance. They teach their crafters how to make simple lavender massage oil (without distilling, which is messy and complicated) by loosely filling a jar with lavender (stems, buds and flowers which have been "bruised" with the fingers to release the fragrance) and filling the jar with almond or olive oil. After it steeps for about a month, it is strained through cheesecloth and decanted into a clean bottle.

Butterflies and Hummingbirds love lavender, as do bees. Deer ignore it, so do ground squirrels, so we plant it between other crops to deter these pests from tomatoes and other edible attractions. Gophers only go for it when there is nothing else to eat.

The afternoon is a good time for harvesting lavender as long there are no bees about. Fáno, of course, can harvest in the midst of a full swarm of bees and think nothing of it. When the rest of us are harvesting, we like to wait until just after the sun goes down, when it's still warm so the fragrance and oils are high, but the bees have gone home.

Harvesting angustifolia is easy, because the spikes are long and straight. You can grab a handful of spikes and snip them off together.

If you bunch the stems and tie up with string or a rubber band, the bunches can be hung in a warm, dark spot for drying. A bunch will dry in about a week.

Fáno and Felix make round little tuffs of the plants when pruning to keep the fields organized and beautiful, as lavender tends to get rangy and woody if left to its own devices.

Mama Maria planted borders of Spanish lavender even though they have no scent because she liked the shapes of the blossoms. Fat and round.

Sweet Farm

Nana's Confession

Nana, Rita and Fox sat at the counter in the Tea Room at 10am with the door locked. A fresh, thick-sliced date loaf sat on the breadboard, a bowl of cream cheese, a jar of apricot jam, three tea cups and a pot of English breakfast tea.

Rita, in her sweet breathless voice, asked, "OK, Fox, Sister, fearless leader of Sweet Farm, what is it to be? What is Chuck's job? Just so we know. I am very fine with it all, and am happy to have Chuck here, but what on earth will he do?"

"Well, first, he'll harvest. We'll all have to harvest. It's been sunny, everything is coming in gangbusters right now, so it's all hands on deck, or, uhm, whatever. Anyway, he can really be of help to Fáno and Felix in the oil and essence production, no matter what he says, but it has to happen now, and I think he'll like it, if he lets himself. After harvest, we'll deal with the rest."

Nana was quiet. She was away, far, far away. She had visions in her mind of a beach, a hut, a sarong, a tan, visions of William. Of...

"Noon?"

"Oh. What?"

"Where were you?"

"Nowhere."

"Uh huh."

"No, really."

"Where were you? You haven't heard a thing we've said all morning. Your mind is on something else."

"What is it?" Rita asked.

Nana looked down at her hands. She scratched her head. She looked up at her sisters with tears in her eyes. She opened her mouth to speak, and stopped. Then she tried again.

"I... I have to tell someone. I have to tell you."

"Tell what, Noons? What?"

"Ah. Uh, I... Oh, crikey, I hate this. But if I don't tell you, I will go mad. I swear it. There is... there is someone."

"Someone what?" Rita asked.

"Someone else! She has a lover! That's what *someone*!" Fox was nosing in!

"Whoa. Really?" Rita asked.

The sisters sat in silence. Four eyes looked at Nana, who studied her cup for a moment and then said, "Yes. Yes, I've had a lover. For about a year. His name is William. He is a tenor. Based in London."

"Well."

"Wow."

"How did you meet?"

"Does Chuck know?"

"Where do you go?"

"What.....?"

"Please, stop." Nana almost laughed. "If this weren't so serious I'd think you two were really funny. No, Chuck doesn't know.

150

We met at a gathering after an opera performance I attended with a Croft & Anderson client. I was invited backstage to the Green Room, and...."

"And what?"

"And, one thing led to another: to William driving me home, William kissing me goodnight, William calling me, making me feel alive, and real, and sexy, and not... dead. Or crazy."

"Where is he now, your William?" Rita whispered.

Nana sniffled through her kleenex, "In Austria, a gig. He's very busy, travels all over the world." The tears, held back for so long, let loose. And Nana, perhaps feeling safe for the first time in years, here with her sisters, in the Sweet Tea Room, in lavender, in the womb, let down... and cried all the tears for all the years she'd held them in.

Through these tears, and in and around these tears, and with these tears, she spoke. "But, it is over, really, it has to be over, if I am going to survive this Chuck business right now. Because if William called tomorrow, I'd chuck Chuck and leave Jolene safe with you and go off with him to... to..."

She wiped her eyes, blew her nose, threw the tissue in the basket on the floor, pulled a stack of fresh tissues out of the box, picked up her tea cup and sipped the hot black tea, letting its steam blur her memories and the beverage warm her veins. She set down the cup, looked at her sisters and, in a voice choked with emotion and with a soul burdened with conflicts and feelings, said, "...anywhere, anywhere, I don't care, I'd just go and have a sweet beautiful life, and forget all this, and stop crying myself to sleep every night because my own life, my marriage, my family, is in ruins."

 Stevie

Aunt Fox gathered everyone to the terrazzo patio behind the Distillery for a lesson in harvesting lavender, as if we didn't know how. But she wanted to make sure the day laborers got it right, and Chuck, of course, who was already freaking out about his precious hands, which, to me, just looked nicotine-stained with raggedy nails—and his cuticles were a mess. It's funny what sticks in your mind.

The patio was imbedded with bits of lavender sea glass touched with mica, something Mama Maria's herb-growing cousin found and shipped to Carmel Valley from France at his own expense. The mica reflected sunlight and the patio twinkled lavender around the farm.

André, the French cousin, couldn't believe Mama Maria really grew decent lavender in Carmel Valley until he visited in the summer of 1957. He also disbelieved that we had a member of a Romani tribe in our midst—being a part of my grandmother's opinionated French family after all—but his visit proved that one to be true, too.

He snubbed my father and treated him like a servant. Rita bristled, so did Aunt Fox. But the ever-mellow Fáno took it in stride, telling my mother, "Be patient weeth your mother's cousin, for he carriez ze ignorance of his ancestors on his back. And eet eez heavy."

André treated my mother like a small child. He patted her on the head, only once—she whacked his hand away like a fly.

"Off!" she said, and gave him the *Don't Mess With Me, Jack* look, for which she was famous, especially dealing with large, condescending people—most everyone from her perspective.

André stayed long enough to get in Fox's way during harvest, too, but he soon learned who was boss when he tried to re-model her drying system—she brushed him out of the barn with the wide end of the broom. Only much later did she admit he had some good ideas.

Now, Aunt Fox was saying, "Place thirty or so rubber-bands on your 'holding wrist,' meaning the hand you'll hold the bundles with, and place the sickle knife in your 'cutting hand,' with which you'll make the slice across the stems. We are cutting bundles today, so please make your stems the same length, about 15 inches, including blossoms. Grab about a 1½ inch thickness of stems, which averages 75 stems in each final bundle.

"Make your cut in a sort of swoop and clip motion, like this," she cut through the stems in her hand with a smooth clean whack, "wrap a rubber-band around the stems like this, low down, 2 or 3 times. Lay your bundle in the basket. You should realize about five bundles per plant."

During this presentation, Chuck tried to listen: smoking, fidgeting, I could tell he was distracted. I watched his hands. When he wasn't picking his cuticles, or gnawing on his nails, he tapped his knee with his fingers. I thought it a random nervous tick, but I soon realized he tapped out tunes. Hard as I tried, I couldn't tell what he tapped, so I imagined that he was calming his mind with *Claire de Lune,* or *Moonlight Sonata,*

I knew he loved songs about the moon, something he and Tate had in common. I wanted him to put down his cigarette and take deep breaths, but I was too young to know the gravity of his crisis and thought there were simple solutions, but there weren't.

Eleven of us were harvesting, so it moved right along. Tate, Jo and I worked together, three to a bush, Felix translated for and directed the hired hands—second or third or fourth or fifteenth cousins of his who had been California dreamin' in Mexico just weeks before. I wondered where they would go on Sunday, when our job was done. I wondered if they had beautiful wives, truant daughters, prodigal sons. I wanted to know how they sent home to their families the money they earned, which is what I had heard all Mexican workers did. I heard from one of my classmates, and thought to be true, that they were all doctors who called themselves Manuel, because manual labor in America earned them about a thousand times more than what they could make in Mexico as physicians. They spoke no English and my Spanish was worse than my French, so I couldn't ask them all my questions.

We developed a humming kind of workforce, each person part of this whispered melody, grabbing, whacking, banding, tossing into the basket. Chuck disappeared during harvest for about three hours and everyone flipped out. I remembered seeing Chuck go off to sit under a tree for a cigarette break: he must have made an escape when no one was looking, because when he came back he had sticks and leaves in his hair and you could have lit his breath with a match.

I wondered, did he have a flask or a bottle in his jacket? Stashed by a tree?

He even yelled at Jolene, which was unusual, because he generally treated her with the most respect he could muster up for anyone. She jumped when he bellowed and knocked over my basket of lavender bundles, which knocked me over, too, and I stumbled into Tate.

Aunt Fox was more than a little angry, since bruised lavender doesn't sell, but Chuck was oblivious. Regardless of this obliviousness, Fox told him to, "Go sober up, you fool." He stumbled into the Adobe and disappeared. The rest of us humming harvesters kept on.

END OF AUGUST 1960

The Hobbit House
Home of the Girl Cousins' Club

The cousins sat on the steps in front of the Adobe, contemplating their clubhouse through the trees, waiting for Fáno to show up, at last. Lavender harvest was over, drying underway, the girls were days away from going back to school, and the rain was a-comin', all of which gave Fáno and the girls the impetus they needed to get this project in the works.

Jolene, fiddling with her hair, finally said, "I don't think we should change it."

"What?" Tate and Stevie said together.

"I mean, yes, we should add room, but can't we think of a way to do it without destroying what you've done? It's so... *so* beautiful, *so* entirely Hobbit-like. If we change it too much, it will lose all its character."

"But what can we do?' asked Stevie. "It's already too small for two people, much less the three of us. We have to do something."

"Well, why couldn't we just take out one wall, the one at the back, and add on? That branch there would hold it. We could use those warehouse boards for the extended deck and for the sides of the, uhm, wing, and then add on some more of that amazing roof stuff, moss and sticks and whatever."

"Hmmm," Stevie said.

"Mmmm," Tate said.

"And, we could make that section a little taller and you could have the old wing, Stevie, since you are the smallest. See, we have enough room there for a T shape, and it gives us each a cubby to put our own stuff in—our little stash of stuff. Tree stuff. Hobbit stuff. A favorite pillow or cards... I don't know. And in the middle, it is clubhouse. I am just saying that I don't think we need to sacrifice what's there already for what we need."

 Stevie

We have boys' names, you know," Jolene said one day while squatting with me on the ground, sanding the boards Fáno would use on our architectural wonder. These weathered ancient slabs of trees, whitewashed many times over, cracks permeated with the dirt, detritus and dust of the Salinas Salad Bowl and her windy farms, were once the walls of a grain warehouse. As we sanded, we found markings and scratches, initials and hearts. Sand blocks in hands, dust masks on faces, we sanded on, and these discoveries kept us going when we otherwise would have flagged or found a reason for another break. We'd brush the sanded debris away and marvel at each sighting: "GB&DG;" a heart with an arrow through it—"Jake" scratched above, "Marla" below.

"What?" I mumbled through my mask. I was thinking about Jake and Marla. The mask was damp with my breath, so I whisked it off for the conversation.

158

"Boys names. Jo. Steve. Tate. It's so perfect. No boys allowed, only we have boys' names. We are up in a tree, not playing with dolls, or crafts or whatever most girls do, and we are sanding these boards and making this ourselves. We are like Girl/Boy Scouts."

 ## Jolene

Fáno sawed off a 1"x12"x24" length of wood from the stack so I could make a sign.

No Boys Allowed

I was blathering on about Boy vs. Girl Scout activities: "Boys go camping and fishing and saving the world while girls sell cookies and... make little bird houses with popsicle sticks. The boys get pocket knives and flashlights and learn about mouth-to-mouth resuscitation and setting bones and stuff, and the girls learn to put bandaids and Mercurochrome on a cut and take your temperature."

"Well, anyway, learning about First Aid is useful."

"Yeah, I know, but boys get to do all the cool stuff like..."

Stevie interrupted my train of thought.

"You're different," she said.

"Than what?"

"Than we thought you'd be." She looked down, and I wondered what she wasn't saying.

"How's that, then?" I asked, although I was afraid of the answer.

"Well, I haven't quite put it in words yet, but, well, we kinda thought you'd be... well, just kinda... a little teeny, weeny bit...."

"What? Geez!"

"Stuck up. There. OK, I said it. I'm sorry. We just didn't know. We thought you'd be more English, more, ah, BRITish. We were so afraid you wouldn't like us, or we wouldn't like you. But..."

My mind raced a million directions. *Stuck up? Me? That's so entirely ridiculous.*

"That's really funny, Stevie. May I call you Steve? I mean it's funny, not ha ha but funny, uhm, what's the word, ironic, that you thought I might be stuck up. About what? My lunatic family? My grades? My hair? Crikey, Steve, I thought you lot would be stuck up, out here in Paradise surrounded by lavender and all kinds of normal life."

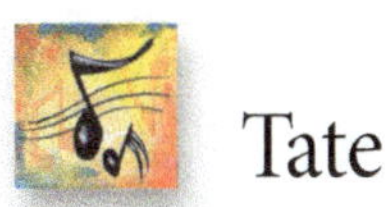 Tate

Blue is the Color I Cry

What do I do when I can't find a song?
What do I do when you're gone?
What is the scheme in this life gone apart?
Where is the light? The fun?
Are you my dad? And where did you go?
These are the questions I'd ask you
I'd ask you right now, if you were here
I'd say, "pretty please" and, "thank you"
I play music all day and it rings in my ear
I hear sounds wherever I go
I remember the sounds the stars used to make
When you rocked me at night, to and fro
You once were my dad, I remember the warmth
But that memory is all that you left me
I await your return, so my heart doesn't burn
But you left me no clue, map, or key
You left me no way to find you, my dad,
My dad, if it really is true
You left no sign or path to walk
Which leaves me nothing but blue
Blue songs in the night, blue thoughts in my head
Blue symbols across the sky
Blue is the color of sadness, my dad
Blue is the color I cry

Where's My Stuff?

"Mum?"

"Mmm?"

"Where's my stuff?"

"What stuff, Jolene?"

"My room full of stuff from London. My things, you know, pillows, stuffed animals, records, letters, clothes. Stuff, Mum! The rocking chair ostensibly once owned by the Duke of Windsor. The dolls Grand Mama brought me from Paris. My Paris Can-Can Dancers Postcard collection. The fuzzy coat from..."

This has gone on long enough, Jo thought. She'd gotten nowhere with her father, but perhaps her mother made some plans before they bolted. No one seemed to care about what they'd left behind. Was there still a flat in London?

"I.. hum... I don't know, really, Jolene." Her mother looked a bit abashed, and tried to look away, but Jolene stared her down. "We left that to your Grand Mama. She, er, volunteered to help close down the flat. It was mostly her furniture, anyway. I... I don't know beyond that. Perhaps I'm a bit preoccupied."

"I'll say," Jolene mumbled under her breath.

"What was that?" snapped her mother.

"Nothing."

"Do you have a problem, Jolene? Have I not handled this to your standards?"

"It's OK."

Jolene sat up in her little cot and wrote a list by flashlight. It amazed her how little there was on the list, but, she intended to write to her Grand Mama Charlotte, just the same.

# Stevie

Chuck lasted about twelve weeks on the farm. Six months later, when Aunt Nana could talk about it, she said they knew they were close to the end of their story, they never spoke it out loud, but she was sure he knew it, too. Even so, the actual ending surprised her.

She thought he would leave and go back to England without her and camp out with his mother—he could do that there, stay in his old room with food and drink delivered, hiding from the world in the safety of his mother's net. Or perhaps Nana would put him in restraints and a hospital for a few weeks, to dry out and come to his senses, if that were at all possible.

Since all of his pockets were empty, he had few choices.

They hardly spent any time together, what with Aunt Nana working more and more hours at The Dream Catcher and Uncle Chuck feigning sleep every time she came into the room, due to that unacknowledged agreement between them to use their favorite mode of mutual survival, silence, in the company of others.

And, Chuck disappeared regularly.

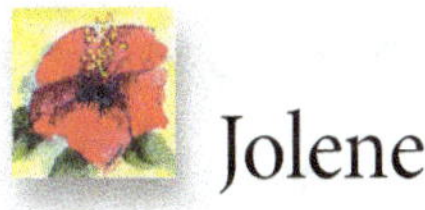 # Jolene

The harvesting scene prompted my parents to call a truce. Nana even got Chuck to slow down the drinking for a few minutes. Maybe for a day.

I overheard them whispering in their bedroom when I got up to visit the loo:

"I am just saying that, for her sake, we've got to try to make a go of it. We need to patch it up here, Charles."

"Uh huh. How's that, Nana? What d'you mean, 'patch it up'?"

"Fix it, Charles. Fix it. Fix us. What can we do to keep our family from disintegrating before our eyes? We are losing each other, losing Jolene, she doesn't even want to be around us anymore. If we are going to survive together, please stop drinking."

"What makes you think I want to survive together? Maybe my flask is a better wife to me than you are. You're no rock, you know." I heard Nana gasp.

"Nice. Really nice. I didn't deserve that, Charles," she said. "I'll pretend that's the liquor talking and not you."

I sensed her moving toward the door, so I scurried into the loo, pulled down my pajama bottoms and perched on the lavender seat.

The next day, he was sober. But he was not at all comfortable in his skin, and was shaking by noon, and by the next day, all his not-so-secret stashes were well supplied.

An Excerpt from Stevie's Honors English Journal 1960s
The Chapel House

Our house has known myriad incarnations: ranch chapel, farmer's office, storage, overnight bunkhouse for hired pear pickers who spread their blankets and bed rolls on the plank flooring and whose idea of heaven was the indoor flush toilet and running water. Never mind the cobwebs and mouse droppings.

Then, Deke Harley moved in when he first came to work at Sweet Farm. He added the outdoor shower, a guy's bogus "kitchen"—hot plate, counters made of boards on saw horses, bricks and boards for shelves lined with cans of Dinty Moore Beef Stew and a styrofoam cooler for bacon and slabs of meat to grill on his little cast iron hibachi thingy—now in the barn, tucked behind the distiller, so Fox won't likely come across it—and a few necessary items: saucepan, spoon, bed, table, rodent traps. He left it to the various and plentiful rodentia in a hurry, though, when he and Aunt Fox created their little nest in the barn, which was shortly after they'd created Tate in the bunkhouse.

It is a sanctuary for us. The cross is long-gone, but the space holds onto something special—"mojo," Fáno says. "Ze Essence of the Creator lingers, everywhere. Eet comes from ze workers, ze spirits, even our old friend, Deke. We zhould disteel eet," he says.

Rita understood right away that Fáno had his eye on the chapel/bunkhouse: for her, for me, his all-of-a-sudden family. Fáno circled the old building in a trance, humming, tracing its frame

166

and corners with the tips of his fingers, running his denim sleeves along the windows, polishing the brass door handle with his red bandana. He sat in the shade of the oak by its front door, whittling fantastic birds out of soft wood and humming in Spanish.

Imagine a box with a peaked roof and spire, about 900 square feet, roughly cut into four parts: Part One, living/dining/kitchen, Parts Two and Three, the bedrooms and Part Four, bathroom/washer/dryer combo. There are three entrances: a sliding glass door on the south side of the living space facing the river; a dutch door in an alcove on the deck on the east side, with a shiny brass handle and a well-worn mat encrusted with Sweet Farm mud; and another slider, into my room.

We tend to roam on the compound from one home to the other. Sometimes we go to Jolene's little Art Box bedroom in the Adobe—nicknamed since she found Poppy's box of pastels and other drawing materials. Instead of having the room painted, she drew trees and leaves and sunlight and shadows all over her walls. The beige in the background is disappearing, covered by bursting color and patterns in nature. Right now, she is plotting out the ceiling: the sky—half day, half night, separated by a half-sun-half-moon in the middle. Jo has surprised us, Tate and me. Jolene says she never drew anything before she tried the pastels, but, we can't believe it. She's still a Londoner, a city girl (at least the tassel loafers have been replaced by Keds and boots), but there's an artist emerging in her, and she looks different.

Or we sometimes go to Tate's Cube in the barn—we hang there the least: it is about as big as a shoebox and overflowing with Tateness—Tate comes with a lot of paraphernalia: a guitar *with case, a recorder, binders of sheet music, a wooden music stand, shelves of books about music, basket of clothes to be washed, basket of clean clothes to be folded, hot roll-ers, a small bed, a stool to sit on for practicing the guitar, and a growing collection of fancy tooled-leather belts with glitzy rhinestone and gem-encrusted buckles displayed on*  *one wall on big S hooks, which now suddenly appear to be hang-ing from a branch of a tree. Jolene looked it up in one of Poppy's books: trompe l'oeil—it means "to fool the eye."*

We like the Chapel best because Tate's mom is always focused on something and trying to get everyone organized, and Jolene's mom is always PO'd at something, or someone, or everyone. But, my mom, Rita? She's making simple syrup and toasting coconut.

When re-doing it from bunkhouse to home, Fáno found Mexi-can tiles out behind the barn and covered the rickety old plank floors. Rita said that as the Chapel House interior walls went up, and the space began to take shape, she would come in and read cookbooks while Fáno was working—she'd sit quiet as a mouse in a corner and listen to him humming while hammering or painting or drawing. He makes things with such love. Rita thinks it's the humming that lingers and makes it holy.

Now see. That's what I mean about them. I don't know any other person who says that about her husband. And he says the same crazy stuff about Rita.

I am sitting now looking at the walls of my bedroom, imagin-ing arches and flowers, maybe a hummingbird.

168

Sweet Farm
The Bucket Day

Pointing to a large bucket of green slimy water sitting half under a wheelbarrow, Fox said, "Oh, no, is that still there? For a *week*, Chuck?"

This was the third time today he'd come under Fox's amber-eyed scrutiny and was found lacking. Chuck tried to remember the last time he did anything right. He turned away from Fox to hide his face, turning blotchy red—his cheeks were hot, his temples burned. It was close to noon, and Chuck trembled for a drink.

But, here in the walkway at the back of the barn, he turned toward Fox with his fists clenched at his side and, with exaggerated chivalry, bowed low and groveled, "Whatever shall we do, Madam? The troll has left the bucket, the bucket is full of water, oh dear! Oh dear!"

But Fox did not sense it coming. Casually, thinking it was an ordinary diversion, one of his efforts to be funny, she said, "Very funny. Please, just empty the bucket, will you? It looks murky, breeding mosquitoes, no doubt—toss it somewhere that needs the water, will you?"

Jock, sitting in his shiny black Cadillac warming it up for a trip to the market, witnessed what came next. He didn't see Chuck's face. He didn't hear the cry of anguish from Chuck's lips. He didn't notice that Chuck's arms were stiff and trembling. But he did see Chuck suddenly pick up the bucket and—just like that!—empty its contents over Fox's orange head, as if she were a bougainvillea.

Then, calm as could be, he dropped the bucket and turned away, headed, surely, toward his rock, where his solace lay hidden in the weeds.

Fox came after him like a cheetah chasing prey. She grabbed Chuck by the arm and pulled him around to face her. "Why did you do that?" she fumed in his face, water dripping from her hair and streaming into her shirt. "What is wrong with you? I asked you to do a simple thing!"

"Because I don't give a fig. Because you looked... parched. Because, this whole place stinks of the freaking lavender and I am beginning to stink, too. Because I hate you, all of you. Go away."

Chuck walked off, leaving Fox stunned, wet and shivering in the chilled October air. Her shirt was soaked through, hair slimy with green water. She held herself in her own arms, feeling bereft and cold.

She thought she was making progress with Chuck, that there was some spark left in him. He and Nana were, if not happy, at least co-existing. They were trying to knit back together the unraveled sweater of their relationship. Trying to keep Chuck sober: a futile idea.

Fox shivered, not quite knowing where to go with this. Jock lurched out of the car and came to her, having yelled out to Chuck with no response.

"What the Sam Hill was that all about?" Jock asked, his gravelly voice high with tension. He put a blanket from the car around Fox's shoulders.

"I, uh, really don't know, Poppy. He, well, he just kind of went off, like he had been building up some steam. I think I was just in the way.

"Or maybe not. Maybe I egged him on—bated him, somehow. He had red eyes, Poppy, filled with hostility. I... uh... I don't know."

 Jolene

The evening after the commotion over the bucket, my father acted like nothing happened. I missed the moment itself, but energy like that lingers in the air, like when someone with strong perfume leaves a room, but you know she's been there. Certain things don't lie.

That reminds me of a night in the London flat with my father. I was coming down the stairs from my room to the living room, and he decided to stumble up, who knew for what: his/ their bedroom was on the first floor, and the only thing upstairs was my room and loo.

Maybe for no reason. Alcoholic cabbageheads need no reasons for their actions, and for no reason, really, no reason at all (I didn't even look at him, I was busy avoiding looking at him by keeping my eyes focused precisely on my tassel loafers), he stopped and grabbed me by the arm.

"Don't look at me like that!" he spit in my direction. "What are you looking at, anyway? Get on up to your room—I'll have a word with you, missy."

He marched behind my back up the stairs, herding me like a goat to its sacrificial destination.

By the time we got to my room, I was shaking. I didn't know what he would do. He'd never actually been violent with me, other than choke-holding me in the dining room one night for mouthing off to Nana about the dishes. Well, I guess that was violent.

But this was different. He threw me up against the wall with no small force. I slid down to the floor into a pretzel shape, collapsing in on myself in protection. I sat motionless on the hardwood floor, shivering and shaking and scared out of my wits.

"Who the f*** do you think you are? You and your snooty mother and your even worse snooty, condescending California grandparents? All this? All this you have here? Is because of me! You are all nothing without me. I am a LORD!"

With that, I knew he was twisted up, because he made us promise to never mention that to our friends, which is hard to hide, when you have to introduce your grandmother as Lady Charlotte. I was petrified.

172

He looked away, and focused instead on my dressing table, where all my little lotions and potions and polishes were neatly placed by size and color. In a flash, before I could react or squeak or yell out for my mother (what she could or would do, I didn't know) he swept his arm across the surface and crashed every little glass bottle and jar and dainty little thing onto the floor into a broken, stinking, oozing heap. The red nail polish ran in a tiny stream on the tile floor, staining the white grout forever.

When he glared at me like that, his face beet-red, his crazy-person mask on, I cringed and put my hands over my head like a wrestler yelling, "Uncle!" He didn't hit me. He had an odd, satisfied look on his still flaming face as he gazed at my floor. But, the high, frenetic energy had oozed away with the mess. He deflated, like a tire. His fury was gone.

He just said, "Clean that up!" and walked out of the room and back down the stairs. Like, "Oh, well, guess I showed her."

And like the day with the bucket, he either pretended that nothing ever happened, or he really did not remember being such a jack ass.

Aunt Fox went into her hole on the bucket day, for which I could hardly blame her. She should have stayed there. It would have been safer.

October 1960
The Dream Catcher Bookshop
Carmel Valley Village
Nana

Nana sat on a low stool in the new Dream Catcher Book-shop in the Village, at the far end of the little plaza. Practically everything in the big open room was made of red-wood—the walls, the bookshelves, some of the furniture. All warm, soft red-brown. She was alone with 20 boxes of books to unpack, code, label and put away in alphabetical order, spine-out except for an occasional face-out—a new bestseller or a hardcover with an attractive cover.

Nana kept stopping to peruse the back covers or the inside flaps and then kept on reading, following her nose.

Beside her on the floor, she stacked books to take home to carefully read without bending the pages back (a perk of the job, in exchange for writing one-paragraph reviews for *The Dream Catcher Monthly Newsletter* to be given away free at the counter). The stack was already a foot high: *To Kill a Mockingbird, Rabbit Run, Black Like Me, Born to Trot, Hiroshima mon amour, Country Girl,* and *The Autobiography of Eleanor Roosevelt.*

She kept reading. Otherwise she would just sit and stew

in her own juices, which were running on empty and about boiled off. She should eat more.

At least while she kept busy at the Bookshop, she wasn't thinking about the situation at home—at Sweet Farm, which was home sure enough, for now. But just now... oh dear, here goes her mind again...

What to do? Chuck needs help, but not from me. I am the last person. I can't bear to sleep next to him. The little couch we brought in so I could read does the trick nicely. I don't mind curling up. He can have the bed.

Our conversations are mono-syllabic. We haven't had sex in months. Crikey, sex! We can't even look each other in the eye, much less kiss or touch.

This time, it's different. It's... I don't know... deeper.

He needs a counselor, or a doctor, or a home for the emotionally and mentally imbalanced. With bars on the windows and plastic forks and dishes.

He needs to be locked away from the bottle, maybe away from me—I certainly need to be away from him.

I wonder if I could get him to an AA meeting. I guess he first has to admit he has a problem. And he certainly doesn't hear me when the subject comes up. Has to be someone else to get through to him. Who?

Crikey. How long will this go on? Am I just babysitting? Enabling? The AlAnon person told me by putting up with it I am just enabling him. Ha. She has no idea.

But, it's more than the booze. It's the whole package. He's a ticking time bomb. Dangerous. Very bad for Jolene. We can't have a repeat of that incident in London last year. I think his weirdness is escalating. Bad. Very bad.

Oh. And here I go, thinking about him again, when I need to get these books on the shelves.

And all this drama, when the reality is, I was mentally packed and ready to gather up Jolene and leave London without him.

Nana rose from her little stool, filled her arms with a tall stack of books in alphabetical order and went to the wooden shelves along the wall: Durrell, Goldwater, Guevera, Pope John Paul II...

The door blew open with the wind, slammed back against the wall and Jock came in. He slowly turned and closed the door behind him.

"Poppy! Where's Fox? We were planning to go to the stables together." Nana set the stack of books down on the oak table and turned to her father.

"Hghmph. You'd best hear the story, and then we'll go home."

"Oh, God."

"Well. You alone here?"

"Yes, Pop. I'm alone. What's happening?"

"It's Chuck, darlin'—"

"Yes, right," she sighed, "It's always Chuck."

And the truth shall make you free
– John 8:32

October 1960

The New & Improved Hobbit House
Sweet Farm
The Truth

 Tate

When the day finally came for the *Truth*, the weather had changed and we were bundled up in soft coats, thick socks, and fingerless gloves. (Stevie's idea, from some artsy book or other she'd read: *Parisian writers and artists wear them!*) She bought cheap gloves at Sprouse Reitz dime store in downtown Carmel and snipped the ends off the fingers. I liked the feeling of them wrapped around red tin mugs of hot lavender-hibiscus tea.

I worried that my Truth would 1) be more weird than everyone's—my dad disappeared into thin air, what is more bizarre than that? And 2) I don't write, except for song lyrics or free-form cheesy poems.

If I squeezed my eyes almost shut when I peered in a mirror, I looked just like Patsy Cline, my idol. I sounded more like Elvis Presley, or what Elvis Presley would sound like if he were a girl; that's what my mother said to me on the day I turned twelve.

She didn't mean anything bad by it, so I emulated Elvis, except the grind, self-conscious about my body, still shaped like a rolling pin with arms and legs.

Yeah, I could sing it, but I could never write a story.

Imagine I'm a girl Elvis. Blonde Elvis. Elvina. I'm all slow and bluesy, and my eyes are half closed. I am wearing a cowboy hat covered with jewels.

My daddy is gone...

My mother is sad...

She lost the best friend...

That she ever had

He up and he left her...

Without a goodbye...

He's gone and his daughter...

Doesn't know why

My mother is lonely...

My daddy's a ghost...

Her tears in the moonlight...

Hurt me the most"

Stevie

I was nervous as a rabbit in a tiger's cage. I don't know why. It was just the Girl Cousins' Club.

We had agreed to bare our souls, in something we called the Truth. Poppy watched me labor over my essay for weeks: hours in his study, looking up synonyms in the thesaurus; sitting on my bed with my journal in my lap, just holding it closed, like if I let go or opened it, the words would spill out all over the floor like pick-up-sticks and I'd have to gather them up and start over.

Poppy gave me this quote for my desk:

Interviewer: *"How much rewriting do you do?"*

Ernest Hemingway: *"I rewrote the ending of* Farewell to Arms, *the last page of it, thirty-nine times before I was satisfied."*

Interviewer: *"Was there some technical problem there? What was it that stumped you?"*

Hemingway: *"Getting the words right."*

Notes in my journal:

T.h.e. T.r.u.t.h.

Steve/Stevie/Stefani

The best things about me:

OK smart enough

Nice—I am good to animals and other living things

I pay attention—I am a good listener

Rita & Fáno are my parents

The Worst Things About Me

I am very impatient

Stubborn

A She-Goat, according to Fáno

Can't subtract

Short

Rita & Fáno are my parents

True Fears

That Rita and Fáno will be so deliriously and intensely happy that they will forget to pick me up at the supermarket or school someday and just flit off to... well, just flit.

Or, that my father's family will finally track me down and take me back to the bosom of the tribe, where all Romani children should be. Although, I've always wanted to know my heritage, so what better way than being stolen in the night!

When other kids imagine monsters under their beds, I see dark hands, reaching out from the dark for my ankles. I hear tinkling bells attached to the necks of restless ponies and caravan trailers.

But, then, I fear that no one will love me because I am little and dark and "undesirable," which is what my grandmother thought before she got to know Fáno. Even the Romani would consider me unclean, tainted by outsiders' blood.

There are obvious contradictions in the above paragraphs, but then, I am on the cusp of my teens, which is probably enough of an explanation.

I know that my situation is different from Tate's or Jo's with their parents, because they have very real fears and losses, I mean, actual drama going on right this minute, physically missing father, emotionally missing pickled father, and I just know what they will be writing in their Truth stories, it's hard not to know, we are together all the time and transmit messages in secret code.

Tate's father is invisible, which I think is worse than if he were dead, because if you know he's dead, then it's final. But invisible means "unseen." Which means he could be just around the corner. Which means he might come back. And no one knows what that would mean.

 # Jolene

Truth notes: My dad's a little cra-a-azy and my mom's made out of glass—this fragile object that looks all hard on the outside but needs to be wrapped in tissue and nestled on a bed of shredded paper.

And I? I am JoJo the clown, the puppet on a string.

Not the world on a string.

What does that mean, anyway?

My Dream:

An Explosion of color

Fragments bursting in the air

We are Puppets: me, my parents

Body parts propelled out or into
*   this vortex of color,*

Mostly red, then purple, then red

Which mixes with my hair, more red

Which mixes with shards of glass
*   and the leaves and trees on my*
*   bedroom walls*

We have two sides to our faces,

Tragedy and Comedy,

Happy and Sad

Thalia and Melpomene

And our strings are all tangled up

 Tate

Lyrics of Truth

The Truths of my matter was this bastard issue, my father was MIA and my mother lost to me in her own little world.

I don't know about her...
Where she is in her life...
I only see lonely and
Forever in strife
I love her, I do, but...
I want to know...
She keeps me at arms length...
Out in the snow
I want my mother...
We both want my dad...
She could hold me forever...
we'd both be less sad

An Excerpt from Stevie's Honors English Journal 1960s Rita, Nana & Fox

The three sisters have very different things to say about Sweet Farm.

Fox, that is, the youngest, the wildest, the one with the longing for an old romance... well, she just wants off the farm. Even ten acres, which seems like nothing compared to, say, wheat farmers in, I don't know, Idaho, it still absorbs time and you have to do chores and you have to get up early. You have to like lavender. And, in our case, you have to like living with a lot of other people.

As a girl, Aunt Fox got up early, and, as she put it, "Split early. I couldn't wait to get out of here every day—high school, boys, camping, hiking, girls' overnights, bowling, whatever it was, I said yes, just to get OUT! And look at me," she said. "Still stuck here. Still here. Still here." She shook her head and got that far away look in her eye. I'd say, she still blames Deke Harley.

Isn't it funny? She's fully in charge, like the General of Sweet Farm, and has her entire being invested in this place, only, she's the one who wants out. In fact, she wanted out before Deke Harley, during Deke Harley, and after Deke Harley. She can't blame Deke that she's still here.

Nana is ambivalent. She can relax about Jolene, because she knows she is safe, and that Chuck could feel safe too, if he wanted to, and maybe they had a chance if they could just focus on each other for once.

But Rita? She's the sister who really loves Sweet Farm. She says it's the Center of Time.

Rita says that when they were growing up, they were the Beautiful One, the Clever One and the Little One.

"It was difficult standing next to my sisters—particularly Nana. She'd glide into the room like Lauren Bacall. Fox was just, Fox: shiny and brilliant. But I hopped in like a little rabbit. Someone, only once, referred to us as Foxy, Roxy and Cottontail. It was embarrassing. Especially since I am the oldest. It was incredibly unfair.

"But I've always known that I'd be the one to live on Sweet Farm all my life. Don't tell Fox or Nana. Fox thinks she'll be the one here to the bitter end, just because she wants out so fiercely, but she won't. And Nana believes Fáno and I should go out into the world and make something of ourselves, which I don't really understand, since it feels like we make something of ourselves everyday, right here."

"Maybe she's jealous," I said.

"Maybe. People hurt when they see happy. But besides all that, don't tell me you could even imagine Fáno in the City. I can't. No. We're here. It's just the way it is."

Truth, Part 2

 Stevie

This is October 20, 1960, and this is me, Stefani Awena Michel, also known as Stevie, or even Steve, or Wena by my dad, for Awena, which means "muse" in Welch.

I turned 12 in September and I believe I have grown as tall as I will ever get, 5' 1". I am taller than my father by a breath of air, taller than my mother by several inches.

I have other nicknames, too, not all good ones. One class-mate started calling me *little gypsy girl*, and it stuck. Do they know how rude that is? Anyway, all they know about *gypsies* is the garbage in the history books. I should write an essay about the real Romani.

I have heard that *gypsies* are dishonest, cruel, stupid, unedu-cated and spawns of the Devil. Really?

The only *gypsy* I know, other than the one-fourth of me, is the one-half of my father, but he is mystical and dreamy, smart: he never went to formal school in France, but learned to read when my mother taught him ten years ago, when she was helping him with his English. He knows a lot of cool stuff.

So, my biggest truth, which is a fear, is that someone will someday hurt me or my family because they think Fáno is low.

Maybe I am doing my parents an injustice by the *forget-ting me at the supermarket* thing. If they bolted to England or

France without me, they'd surely remember to call Poppy or Aunt Fox to pick me up and take care of me until they came home. Or until I was sixteen and could drive and take care of myself. And surely they'd send postcards. This does sound pitiful.

I am part French Romani, French but not French; part French-French, since my grandmother is all Frenchified down to her pink garter belt, and my father's father was French; and part Welch: my great grandparents on Poppy's side were both Welch.

All this foreign blood aside, I was born in the Adobe House, pretty much exploding into the arms of my father, who barely had time to wash his hands, much less call the doctor before my mother blurted out a yelp from her lips and a push with her hips and a wet living thing that was me. That makes me a California girl, a true Carmel Valley girl.

The fantasy me will grow up and marry someone sweet and charming like Fáno and sit in my study and write stories and poems all day while I watch my children play in the backyard with a little red rubber ball and a stick.

The real me expects to go to college and earn a degree so I can sit in a classroom on a sunny day, wishing I were out lying in the grass with my non-existent boyfriend, soaking up rays. Instead, I will be teaching conflicted, cynical students how to make sense of themselves and the world, while I write cheap supermarket thrillers at midnight after grading papers dull as dirt. I see Poppy's influence here.

Sometimes I think the world is crazy and will go to war again or the soon-to-be-elected next American president will jump in to save people from their crazy selves, and I will be patching up soldiers on a battlefield with Mercurochrome and bandaids.

I have a recurring dream that I am trying to stop the bleeding on a soldier's chest with a bandaid that popped out of a box of Girl Scout Tagalongs, like the prize in a Cracker Jacks box. The bandaid was stamped with "Be Prepared." The blood kept gushing.

Maybe the real Truth is somewhere in between my imagination and the journey."

 Jolene

After Stevie read her thing, no one said a word for about 60 seconds, which seemed like a day.

Stevie could actually get quiet and focus-in long enough to get all her thoughts in rows and sequences and come up with paragraphs that were beautiful and made sense.

My thoughts get all fragmented and eventually appear in jumbles of color. Words do not come easily.

Something happened overnight, when I left England and got plunked down in Carmel Valley. I went from scrambled thoughts and recurring anxiety attacks to Poppy's pastels on the walls and cans of paint and beautiful soft brushes. This discovery reassigned my constant life review from my brain to my hands, and turned my room into... an empty canvas, awaiting color.

After a short preamble-apology for not being able to *write* my Truth, I showed my work to my cousins. I held my breath, hoping they would *get* the story and not be disappointed that I was a failure in the words department. What can I say? This was more me.

The canvas was 18" x 24"—small enough to fit into the new and improved Hobbit House, but, looking back, not big enough for its subject. Were I to do it again, it would fill a wall.

I thought my puppets were stunning: how their body parts exploded into shards while their intact two-sided faces maintained enigmatic happies and sads. The center of the cyclone was deep purply red, which burned into orange and yellow flames toward the edges of the canvas where you could see the strings that tangled around all of us beginning to singe from the flames. If you looked really close, got up to the brush strokes and color separations, you could see flecks from the broken glass body of my puppet mother. I got the idea from the terrazzo patio floor. I used thick gesso to hold the shards, which I retrieved from the trash.

All the red was intertwined with the red Hibiscus flowers in my hair, petals aflame. For Stevie, I put in a peacock feather. For Tate, I glued on some rhinestones.

It wasn't *all* dark and gloomy. I painted the rims of the canvas bright, bright yellow. I don't know what it meant to them, Tate and Stevie, or anyone else who ever saw it, but the yellow represented the future, the sun coming out tomorrow, a new day, and maybe a new beginning. A flower might grow.

Just to prove that I wasn't entirely without hope. That was true, too.

 Tate

I remembered Jo telling us about the dream several weeks earlier, about how spooky and vivid it was, how she couldn't get it out of her mind. It made me feel better, in a way, that she chose paint instead of words: better about my cropped lyrics and chopped up poem fragments that became *my* Truth.

I played my guitar for about three minutes and then spoke/ sang/chanted my whole Elvina stream of consciousness poem, that ended like this. When I was finished, we were all three in tears.

I'll grow up without him...
He'll never know me...
he'll not know my songs or...
climb in my tree...

This life of a singer...
I love and I hate...
I want now to grow up...
But I'll have to wait...

For what, I do not know...
there's nothing quite clear...
it comes and it goes now...
the knowledge I fear...

I'll grow up without him...
he'll never know me...
he'll not know my songs...
he'll never know me...

He'll never know me...

He'll never know me.....

An Excerpt from Stevie's Honors English Journal 1960s
The Heart

You could say that the Sweet Tea Room and I were carried to term by the same woman at the same time: in womb and brain. So I guess that makes us twins. Milk siblings, because I am sure I gave up precious breast time to the Tea Room, even though Rita carried me in a kangaroo-style pouch in front when she was making bread or rolling out pastry dough—photos of my floury head prove it.

The Sweet Tea Room idea came from my mother's impressions of post-war England and France. If she heard it once, she heard it a thousand times during her tour as an aid to British nurses: "What you need is a nice cup of tea!" It was the cure for everything from pre-wedding jitters to post-war party hangovers, from the common cold to grief.

Later, in France, she discovered the croissant, and that was that. She stayed in Paris long enough to improve her French and learn that a good Puff Pastry has 729 layers of dough and 729 layers of butter. And to find Fáno. And to make me.

If Lavandula is the center of gravity at the Sweet Farm, Sweet Tea is its heart.

 Stevie

Chuck scotch-taped himself together and Nana floated through her days, filling hours with book reviews and poster ideas; they did not spend time in the same room. Mama Maria and Poppy hid out in their quarters, planning an extended cruise. Fáno, in overalls and a green and yellow plaid flannel shirt, his red bandana tied around his head to keep his hair and sweat out of his eyes, was distilling, trying to get the taped-up Chuck to not burn himself on the steam.

The bucket of water was the last hostile act that Chuck staged. Well, maybe second to last. He was spoken to harshly by Poppy, persuasively by Nana, subliminally by his introverted daughter, and not at all by Fox. She was too busy, what with harvesting, bundling, distilling, packaging, bottling and all.

They stayed out of each other's sight for a few days, then Chuck finally made awkward apologies, not believing for one minute he had done any such thing as what they all said he did, but he apologized just the same for being a jerk. Fox looked away.

"So. Really. I *am* sorry. I am out of line. Let's make up and all that and let bygones be bygones." When I heard about that, it didn't sound too apologetic to me.

Chuck was doing it all at the request of others, *he* didn't see why he should give up his little gin crutch! It was the only thing that got him through the slow passage of time in his

198

messed-up head, not to mention calming his jitters and soothing his ragged nerves, therefore his heart was not in the apol-
ogy, the promises, or the very thought of sobriety.

He didn't blame Nana. I remember his blurting out to Rita
in my presence (I could make myself invisible to people like
Chuck) that Nana was a goddess whom he did not deserve. I
think he feared and worshipped her, and kept up this pretense
of hating her because he loved her too much to try to keep her
and never truly believed that she was his anyway. Or something like that.

Then, Chuck discovered Fox.

Discovered is not the right word. It was a complete turn-
around, an uncomfortable one, at that.

He needed something from her, maybe. Absolution?
Forgiveness? No one was sure. But, he suddenly and irratio-
nally began following her with his eyes, like trying to figure
her out, dissect her soul. He brushed his hand against hers, accidentally on purpose. He offered her the salad first at dinner,
the choice cut of meat.

Fox ignored this. Fox ignored most everything that didn't
have to do with lavender cultivation and its attendant business issues. Fox's life was carefully tended, like a plant. She ate,
drank water, got plenty of exercise just moving from place to
place on the farm and doing her share of garden work. But,
her interpersonal relations were... shallow. Wrapped in plastic.
Uncultivated. Fox had no trouble keeping Charles at the same
distance as everyone else. Easier, in fact, because she didn't like
him much.

The Wyman clan, holding onto the calm in the center of a hurricane, went about their individuals businesses like patients in Bedlam: wary, waiting for other shoes to drop. Wymans went through the motions, Huffingtons operated in silence, Michels whispered secret protective chants to the Divine, Roriguezes grounded the whole shebang with solid goodness and a fabulous lack of dramatic enterprise.

Watching. Waiting. Holding the collective Sweet Farm breath.

Death was a friend, and sleep was Death's brother
–John Steinbeck, *The Grapes of Wrath*

November 1960

A Meeting in the Middle
Sweet Farm

 Stevie

To this day, no one knows if it was a suicide note.

"I am so sorry" was all he wrote, and no one is exactly sure when he wrote it. He did not sign it. Fox found it on the desk in the Sweet Farm office.

When the sheriff arrived at 10am, he said there had been "an accident" at Bixby Bridge: that a 1949 VW, and Charles, were found on the wet sand, 280 feet below.

It involved no other car, and he appeared to have been driving quite fast. It happened sometime in the middle of the night. There were no witnesses. "A canyon resident heard the crash," the sheriff said. "He thinks your husband was dead on impact."

Nana stood in stunned silence, mixed emotions creating a soup of her brain, tears held back by guilt and remorse, all of which rendered her as still and cold as an ice sculpture.

Fox discovered the note in Chuck's handwriting earlier that morning, but kept it to herself, not exactly knowing for whom it was intended, or why, or where Chuck was at that precise moment. He was late, as usual—at 8:30, half an hour late. She had not seen him since dinner the night before, when he was abashed and apologetic for his latest transgression. No one had yet noticed the missing VW Split Window Sedan. Except Jolene, who wasn't talking.

Fox thought at the time, maybe the note was for her: he was apologizing again for bad behavior.

But, maybe the note was for Nana: *After all, she is the victim here, not I,* she thought. *I am just here, a convenient distraction from his problems.*

And what a prodigious bundle of problems. No wonder that Guy Templeton walked. Chuck is out of control, disconnected.

Now, in the Adobe with the sheriff, she thought, *The note must be for Nana. What did it mean, though: I am sorry I hurt you? Sorry I almost kissed your sister? Sorry I am going to take the car now and wreck it while killing myself?*

Well, she'd have to show it to them. She couldn't conceal evidence.

"There is a note in the office," she said vaguely to the people in the small gathered circle: the two officers, Maria, Jock, Nana, Rita, Fáno, and three mystified young girls, holding hands. Jolene stood still, with wild horses rampaging through her endocrine system.

"What?" shot back Nana, at the same time the officers turned to Fox and said, "A note? Where is it?"

"I'll get it," Fox croaked, and went over to the office and back without breathing.

Nana grabbed the note from her and choked while reading it. She threw it to the floor and fled to her room. Jo, separating herself from her cousin anchors, ran after her mother.

A silence followed while one of the officers picked up the note, read it, passed it to his associate who read it and gave it to Rita, next to him.

One officer said, "Is that his handwriting?"

A white-faced Rita whispered, "Yes, yes," as she handed the note to Fáno. "What does it mean, though? To whom is this written? And when?"

No one could answer.

Chapter Three
Aftermath

NOVEMBER 1960

Sweet Farm Office

The dust had settled from the horrifying realization that Chuck was gone. It was not a practical joke, it was real. He was gone. No more Chuck.

Although nothing ever "happened" between them, Fox felt guilty over how close she and Chuck came to kissing. She didn't know what came over her in the moment. It was in the air on the compound for several weeks: new delicious strange torment for Chuck, powerful denial and sadness in Fox, a slow-burn fury in Nana. *So weird*, Fox thought. *Chuck and I don't even like each other. Didn't.* But she did lean toward him when she felt his breath on her neck.

Jolene curled up in a ball in bed, speechless; Nana sat in her room in the rocking chair, staring out the window, rocking, rocking; Tate and Stevie sat on pillows in the tree house cutting out stars to put in Charles's grave.

It was quiet on the compound, since no one could speak to the loss, the impact, the grief, the sudden tragic end of almost three months of dramatic tension. Just whispers and brief requests were heard: pass the butter, where are the scissors, do you have tape.

Farley's father picked us up in his jeep. We had to coax Jolene out of her bed and practically dress her ourselves while convincing her that Farley was a reasonable distraction, that being out in the sun in Salinas would be a good thing. For all of us.

Jock and Maria were napping, Rita baking, Fáno distilling.

Fox slumped in the office chair.

Nana came in, not confrontationally, not at first. She came with a question. A hurting in the pit of her stomach, serious question that only Fox could answer. Nana knew that if she didn't get this out of her body she would blow into a billion fragments and break everything in her explosive path.

She looked so calm on the outside, but her insides were torn apart. Her bobbed salt and peppery hair, big eyes, tall erect posture, belied the broken heart. She was rigid with heat, like when you have a fever and it is burning you up all over and slowly steaming through your skin. She was boiling over. It blended poorly with grief.

Fox looked up as Nana walked in the back door. Nana hadn't left her room in the Adobe for about 36 hours, so Fox was surprised to see her showered, made-up, riding breeches and boots on, riding crop and hat in gloved hands, obviously on the way to November Ranch to ride. She'd taken up dressage in England and kept her fragile self together by teaching a horse to obey her subtle body signals, performing precise movements in a ring. She needed it: the outfit, the whip, the control, the precision.

Fox sat at the desk and looked down for a moment. There must have been an audible sigh, perhaps from both women.

Fox looked up.

"Hi." she squeaked. A silence filled the room with its explosive nothingness. Both women's minds were racing. Nana's jaw line flexed. Fox's tail curled under.

"Hi," replied her sister, not as calm as she appeared.

"Want to talk?" Fox asked, feeling trapped down her hole, looking up at the point of an arrow, held by a wild and crazy huntress who happened to be her beloved sister.

"Yes," said Nana, through gritted teeth.

"Sit down," Fox said. Nana ignored the invitation and stood in the doorway with her arms crossed over her chest, riding crop quivering in the crease of her armpit.

Fox stood, faced her sister and said, "I am so sorry, Nana. I don't know what or how this happened. Chuck meant nothing to me. I am so sorry."

"I don't believe you. And if I did believe you, you're telling me that all this happened, and he meant nothing to you? If you didn't like him, what was the bloody point? Why did you do this? *How* could you do this?"

"I didn't *do* anything. Honestly. We were just playing a piece for four hands, and he leaned over the piano and started to kiss me, out of the blue, just as you walked in the door. That's all. Really. I had no idea. I had no designs on Chuck."

"My husband is dead because of you, Fox. Dead."

"No. No. You don't believe that, Nana. You can't!"

"Can't I? How do you explain the rest? The fact that he whispered to *you*, left *you* a note, drove away from here and... and... drove away from here in that ratty $400 car that we'd saved every blasted penny for. He drove away and... he drove away, Fox. He's dead. He's gone and I can't even say I am sorry. I can't ever tell him that I know he did the best he could."

They both started crying at this point, each turning slightly away. Fox caved first.

"Please," she said, and reached out for her sister.

They sobbed for a while and wiped each other's tears and Rita came in from the Sweet Tea Room at the sound of her sisters' raised voices. Soon they were in a three-way embrace that lasted about a decade, until they sat down on the small patch of floor, cross-legged, knees touching.

Fox said, "Nana, I had nothing going with Chuck. This is the truth, Sister. We spent time together, yes, because he worked for me, and playing music was better than hating each other.

"But he was screwed up, Nana. Something was wrong with Chuck, only we didn't know how bad it was until it was too late. He was missing you and hating himself and coping with it all with gin—you weren't around. He snuck drinks, I know he did. How could he not? I wasn't having an affair with Chuck, and if he projected something on me, it was more than I was prepared for. I thought I was beginning to understand him, that's all. I thought... I thought I could help. And besides, you don't know that that note *was* for me. I just found it. I don't even think it was a note about this—about suicide. We don't know that for sure. All it said was 'I'm so sorry.' It could mean anything."

"It means he's gone," Nana sobbed. "He left the note in your office. What should I think?"

"It's not *my* office, honey. It's Sweet Farm's office. It's everybody's office. We are all in here at some point or another. Maybe he was starting a note and gave up. Maybe the note was to you. Maybe he was saying I'm sorry to you, Nana. Then, he just lost it. He imploded. We should have seen it coming."

Rita, who had been quiet, said, "We did see it coming, we just didn't know what IT was."

 Stevie

W e mapped out a neat circle right in the center of the center of the Hobbit House and declared it *Switzerland*, neutral territory. Our own Middle.

"So," I said, "no matter what, we'll meet here and it will be OK. You can say anything, confess major truancies, lies, fears and secrets and it will never pass our lips or these doors or windows. Your secrets are safe with the Girl Cousins' Club."

As it was, Tate and I spent much time alone together in the Hobbit while the family of Lord Charles Huffington contemplated his death. Jo was back in her bed, hugging her stuffed bear. I felt guilty for what I'd said in my Truth Essay about being dead—that it would have been better if Tate's father were *known* to be dead because then it would be final and therefore easier to accept than an unsolved mystery.

I ate my words.

So, which was worse: your dad being MIA, your dad being an outcast, or your dad being dead?

My vote was *dead*.

210

 Jolene

I turned my painting, The Red Vortex, to face the wall, but I kept seeing my dad exploding into pieces and then wondering if he exploded on impact. No one would tell me. All I could see at night was my painting coming to life and all of us blasted to smithereens in the starry sky. Weird to think that my dream became a painting which became a dream but was partly real.

And the bit about the yellow around the edges? A new beginning? The sun will come out tomorrow? Geez. What kind of new beginning was I hoping for?

I kept his secret. But, why was he going south? He said he had a train to catch.

Did I kill my dad?

I kept his secret... But every day, I thought, "Should I tell them?"

 Tate

We waited for Charles's mother, Lady Charlotte, to arrive. She would be in Nana's room, Nana in Jo's room, and Jo to the Chapel House to bunk with Stevie on her little foldout sofa bed in the corner. And me, too.

Jo's brilliant Hobbit House remodel, making it T-shaped, with a communal space in the middle, gave us each a little cubby. I took the time to settle in. I had a little basket. In it I kept guitar picks and several sets of strings, a red bandana, a book of chords, and a sequined top I planned to wear in 1968 at my debut at the Holiday Inn Lounge in Monterey with my country band, Tate and the Boys. In 1968 I would be 21. I had eight years to find the boys, not to mention fill out so I could keep up the little tube top thingy.

And, so much for my Truth being the worst.

 ## Stevie

Tate and I cut out a thousand stars and moons for Chuck, waiting for Jo to return to the Hobbit. All our pique with Chuck dispersed into the air once he was no longer alive.

We moved on to musical notes, carefully drawn in black magic marker in easy-to-cut circles.

We thought about what to say at his graveside.

We heard about some family conflict (this could only mean Charlotte and Nana) regarding where Chuck was to be buried. What did Charlotte want to do? Ship his body overseas? Geez.

Meanwhile, Chuck was in cold storage at the funeral home in Monterey, awaiting his mother's arrival, and no further plans were made.

Charles's mother, Lady Charlotte Grace Huffington, flew into town for ten days. She was a big woman, almost 6 feet

212

tall, with wondrous chest and hips. Her hair fluffed all over her head, a breath of blurry white. Every day, no matter what we were doing, Lady Charlotte trussed herself into one of several, tastefully dark two piece suits, a pink or white or tan silk blouse, each with attached silky ties that flopped over her bosom.

Bosom *is* the word. These were not "boobs." Even "breasts" don't fit this image. It was the archetypal matronly bosom of grandmotherhood, as pictured in every nursery rhyme and story of old times.

And stockings, and sturdy, thick high heels.

Often, a hat.

Oooh, the hats. She let me look in her hat box—one side pocket for feathers and one for clip-on silk flowers and birds and things. Really. Pictures of hats with combinations of adornments lined the lid.

I admired her three sets of pearls, too: short strand for day, medium length for quiet family evenings, and a long rope that wrapped around several times for formal occasions and the "theatah." What did she think we'd be doing? I wondered which pearls she would wear to the funeral, if we had one.

Pancake make-up and ruby red lipstick set off that white powder puff on her head.

Oh, my, she was delicious. In my memory, she is the twin of

Barbara Cartland, the English novelist. Only not so pink. And probably taller.

I admired Barbara Cartland. She looked after the Romani in her neck of the woods and tried to get them better education and permanent homes.

I made excuses to be with Charlotte, so I could study her clothes and... just how *did* she bend down to pick up something off the floor? She had a servant at home to do all her snaps and buttons, I imagined, and, well, all the picking up, too.

It took her a good hour to get ready in the morning. I considered offering my services while she was in Aunt Nana's room for the ten days, just for the experience (Oh, that's a lie! I wanted to see her undergarments!) but, I would probably catch her skin in a zipper or spill the perfume.

She didn't want that, anyway. I respected her for even trying to fit into life on Sweet Farm. Her son was dead, and here she was across the water, fully dressed for high tea with the Queen and was instead on her way to a funeral home in Monterey with my aunts and mother, all in jeans and cotton shirts, to bicker over the body of the dear departed Charles, iced down since Tuesday. Mama Maria tagged along at the last minute, leaving sequestered reverie with her husband to put in her two cents regarding the proper disposition of Chuck's remains, and her mother-hen wings around Nana.

I liked Charlotte: she was crazy about Fáno—she said he was *yare.* You would think that La-a-a-a-ady Charlotte Huffington, of the London Huffingtons, would look down her be-jeweled lorgnette at a you-know-what.

 Jolene

My grandmothers avoided each other like reverse magnets. It had something to do with a hissy conversation at my parents' wedding about abolished European titles—and they hadn't spoken since.

I liked my Grand Mama Charlotte, though. She was stuffy in the English sense, and corrected my grammar ("they don't speak the King's English in the States, you know..."), but she was steady on and helped make sense out of my otherwise screwed up life. She gave me *The Hobbit*, which had become important.

Her other son was dead, her husband died before Nana met Chuck, and now Chuck was gone, too. I felt sorry for her, because she would truly be alone now, if we stayed in the States and ruined our English.

But worse, what would she say if I told her the truth?

 Stevie

Mama Maria's style was long sensible skirts, no petticoats, just a same-length, split silk slip, with checked or dark shirts, tucked in and belted, and the ubiquitous boots of Sweet Farm life. Sometimes she wore cotton socks or kind of heavy stockings and, honest to Pete, a garter belt. I never saw my grandmother in pants. If needed, she tucked her skirt hem into her belt and just kept going.

My grandmother, after twenty years in California, and twenty-something years before that in Ohio, cared little of her aristocratic ancestors or even any of the displaced's off-spring except cousin André.

She said that Lady Charlotte was, "Over ze top. Ask her to step down off her throne for ze one moment." Her accent was more extreme when she was upset.

The bee in Lady Charlotte's bonnet was over the stupidity of the long dead French aristocrats who flaunted their excesses and decadence, thereby forcing a revolution of the starving common people. Who then, as we know, stripped the French glitterati of their titles, privileges, heads and whatnot.

Maria thought Charlotte was a "cream puff" and "rude." The *privileges* of the current English peers were limited to dining rights in the House of Lords, anyway, according to Jolene. So, big deal. Who really cared about this? It was a silly and empty feud. I wanted them to be friends and was secretly trying to effect a truce.

 Tate

I secretly knew that Lady Charlotte thought we were hicks and heathens.

 Jolene

Some things are just inexplicable.

I asked myself unanswerable questions.

Like, "Why did this happen?"

And, "Where did he go?"

And, "Did I kill him?"

But, some things are just inexplicable.

People said, "Oh, he's with you always," and "He's watching over you now," or "He'll always love you."

I didn't buy it.

I mean, my dad was gone, and I didn't think he was a shadowy ghost standing next to me saying, "Hey, Poppet, wanna go for a stroll?"

If so, what's the point of his being there if you can't hear or see him?

What I really thought was that he is now a part of everything, from dust motes to rain, hiccups to laughter, everything.

I worried constantly that someone would find out I let him go. That it was my fault. It gave me a stomach ache to think about our conversation, that no one heard us, that I could go to my own grave with his secret still inside me. Just to keep, as it turned out, my final promise to my dad.

I could have told. He didn't say to me, "Don't *ever* tell." He said, "Don't tell."

But, I knew I had to do it, because all he wanted was to get away and be himself. Find his Super Conductor.

Why did he turn left and go down the coast and not north to the train? I don't know. He could have just snapped. Or he could have been lying to me.

Telling my mother would help nothing. It wouldn't bring him back. And it might make things a lot worse in the aftermath.

But then again, I was withholding information. Would there be a smear on my father if they think it was suicide because that note proves it?

I worried over not liking my parents. It was true. I did not like them. But the reason that I did not like them, was that I could not trust them. It had nothing to do with love.

But when someone you love dies, all you think about is the love. And the grief is that much deeper because of the not liking them.

Does that make sense?

Was I guilty of murder?

Stevie

Jo thought Chuck's death was her fault.

I thought it was because she overheard her parents talking: her mother guilt-tripping him into staying together when he really didn't want to. For her—Jolene.

So, if he'd left, he might have lived. Because, if he'd left, there would have been no more ambiguity. He could have stopped love-hating Nana, and maybe he really could have stopped drinking—wasn't he drinking because he was so unhappy? And he was unhappy because of her, Jolene.

And more like that.

But, as it turned out, he did leave. And where did that get him?

I didn't know everything.

Nana eventually blamed herself (for not being a better wife, and for William, even though Chuck never knew about William). Fox blamed *her*self (the near kiss). Even Jock took some of the rap, for giving Chuck an ultimatum. Everyone on the compound felt guilt, remorse, sadness and loss.

Lady Charlotte

Lady Charlotte wondered just what was going to happen here. Everyone looked shell shocked.

Not she. She saw it coming years ago, and knew young Charles wasn't any more up to the task of living a whole and solid life than was her husband, Lord Charles. Now there was a pansy.

They were just alike, Charles and the senior Lord Charles: the bottle, the mysteries, the dark side, the fantasies.

And her other boy, Rafe, got blown up in a warehouse in the war. He was hiding, Rafe was. Shameful.

But Jock, there, he's a real man. A man's man: well-read, handy, head on shoulders. Why couldn't she have married a man like that?

But, nooo, she married a lunatic Lord with secrets.

Now, all she had was a half-American granddaughter who mystified her, a confused American daughter-in-law who annoyed her and a list of dead Englishmen, all of whom failed her...

And this motley crew.

But she owed them this conversation, at least. Then, she might never have to see any of these people again as long she lived. Enough of this secrecy, this show. There are no more Huffingtons to care. Except this young girl, right here on this little farm.

"Now, then," she began, as the adults gathered in the Middle for the conference about her Charles. Chuck's remains. Almost everyone was there, but no one was talking: Maria kept her eyes on her knitting; Nana swirled Cold Duck; Jock busied himself at the bar sorting peanuts; Rita and Fáno sat on the fireplace hearth holding hands.

Fox dragged her feet in her apartment, wishing she didn't have to be a part of this little confab.

The three girls lay on the bed in their grandparents' room. It was a warm day. No fire muffled the sound between the rooms.

Lady Charlotte leaned toward the family group from her chair and whispered, "Tell me what happened," as if she were in the theatre, asking her partner about the plot of this play.

No one spoke for a moment, but Jock turned around and held up his hand, as if to say, "I'll take this one."

He faced Charlotte, who did not take her eyes off him as he told the story, even when Fox came in the door, poured herself a glass of wine and sat down on the window seat, for Jock spared no detail, and even spoke to his own horror over what part he might have played—had he been an ass to make things tough for Chuck?

Charlotte, waiting for an opening, finally said, with a bit of a choke in her voice, "No, no, it was no one's fault. I should have told you long ago, Nana, but I've never been sure. It was in his genes, I think. His blood. His chemistry, as it is. I don't know. They all die young."

"Who dies young, Charlotte?" Jock was curious, now.

"The Huffington men. It's no one's fault."

She said, "I never told Charles, or Rafe, but their father did not die of pneumonia. He offed himself in the attic when the boys were away at school. He was flighty, hard to manage, squandered Huffington money, always had a drink in his hand, and got into cocaine in the 30s, how he came by it, I'll never know. I was afraid young Charles would go the same way, he could have, with his musical contacts, but I don't believe he did.

"I never met the grandfather, my husband's father was dead before we married, but rumors abound concerning his erratic behavior, and, of course, mysteries surrounding his death. And his brother's death as well. Chuck said you could never be an artist and a Lord at once, so he kept trying to push it off on Rafe, but it doesn't work that way, you see, so we let it drop. It wasn't important. And then Rafe got himself killed. Young idiot.

"No. No one is to blame. I see it now. It was just a matter of time. It's the reason I tried to keep him close. I am afraid that is why I protected him."

Jolene

I could hear the family skeletons rattling as Grand Mama Charlotte pulled them out of the closet one by one. Lying on Mama Maria's bed gave me the advantage of not being seen, but Grand Mama Charlotte's disembodied voice sounded cold and removed, as though she had practiced this speech during the long hours on the flights from London to San Francisco. I knew the interminable length of that journey; she had plenty of time to get it right.

I felt even more sorry for her now.

I couldn't tell right away if my mother was mad that Grand Mama didn't tell her about this mysterious habit of dying young, or if she, Nana, was happy that *she* wasn't entirely responsible. Or if she believed this simplistic story at all.

Any way you looked at it, though, my dad was dead.

Did Grand Mama really think it was inevitable? Did that make it inevitable *and* inexplicable?

And what about *my* part in this disaster? Maybe it *wasn't* my fault. Entirely.

Later That Evening

Lady Charlotte said, "It's unconventional, I know, but we'll do it. It's the only way we'll put this boy to rest. He *must* come to England, it is his home, he had no great love of your country."

"His widow and his daughter are in America, Charlotte," Jock said.

"Yes, yes. Yes, I know. For now."

At the end of the long day wrangling over Chuck and exposing his family dispositions, Lady Charlotte and Jock sat by the fire in the Middle, sipping sherry from thin glasses etched with roses. Nana, Rita and Fox were piled on the bed in Fox's room in the barn like puppies, whispering, Fox and Nana having called a fragile truce, both equally mystified.

Maria rested. *Enough of Lady Charlotte for one day, s'il vous plaît.*

The young girls were planning the memorial with Fáno in the Chapel House kitchen.

"So, it's settled, then," Charlotte said. "Charles will be cremated Monday and I shall take half of him to London."

"And on Wednesday, we will bury the other half here at Sweet Farm. Does this sound morbid to you, Charlotte, in the end, or am I over-reacting? I shudder to think of the unsettled feeling of being in two places at once. And I admit I have no experience with this ashes thing."

"That's why they call it 'Remains,' Jock dear. Or "Cremains," but I find that offensive. The ashes are not Charles, but what is left of our dear Charles's inert body. Charles doesn't need it, or give a fig what we do with it. Perhaps we can put on the tombstone, 'Here lies half of Charles Huffington—the other half rests in peace in Carmel Valley, California.' And you can do the reverse." She paused for a moment. "I am sorry, Jock. I am rarely so crass."

"Understood. He's your son. You've got to crack, sometime. Have you cried yet?"

"No. How did you know?"

"Ah. You have a readable English face: you try to keep a stiff upper lip, and all that. But I can see through the little cha-rade. I mean no disrespect—it's just a fact. Charles tried, but he wasn't good at it, either."

Lady Charlotte's silk slip rustled as she squirmed in her chair. She said, "Hghmph. No. I'll save the tears until I return to London. Perhaps I'll spill a few good ones in the pr-r-rivacy of my roo-o-oms. There's been enough raw emotion here for one day. I'd like to ask Jolene to come home with me, Jock. What do you think? Am I pushing it? She could stay with me and go to Woolsley. I know she wants to board, so perhaps we could..."

Jock held up his hand, "Talk to Nana then talk to Jolene. I want all my girls here, but it is not my decision this time." He thought he knew what Nana would say ("Ho no!") but he was not sure about Jolene.

Lady Charlotte knew that Jolene would come back to London with her. *How could she not? Jolene loves London. Why would she ever want to stay here?*

226

The Rock

On Monday, the cousins walked down Schulte Road. Jolene pulled the red wagon, her hair waving tight red kinks in the breeze and sparkling in the pale November sun. The red wagon carried a large trowel, the green blanket from the Hobbit, two empty grocery bags and three bottles of Coca Cola. Each girl had a 

backpack with sandwiches, and a walking stick, whittled and carved with stars and other symbols by Fáno while he sat under his oak tree during siestas. The sticks were to fend off big cats and coyotes, if it ever came to that.

Jolene had come across Chuck's notebook Saturday night in the piano bench: she rifled around in there looking for his favorite music for Tate and her guitar for the cousin-planned Gathering. Jo held the notebook and a few sheets of music like a monk hugs an open prayer book, close to the chest, and walked back across the yard to Stevie's room, where her cousins waited.

"Wow. Where've you been?" Stevie asked. "That took, like, forever!"

Jo handed Stevie the notebook with Chuck's signature on the inside cover. "These are his last words, other than *the note*. I couldn't move for about ten minutes."

Actually, his last words were the secret, but this is close enough.

"Wow, again," said Stevie. She looked up at her cousin. She handed the book to Tate, who looked through it, humming.

The girls took turns reading the poems aloud. When they got to "My Peaceful Willows," they were in tears, and the cousins figured they were onto something.

> *This rock is where I find my peace*
> *The bridge protects me from all eyes*
> *The willows are my tender friends*
> *The moon shines in the starry skies*
> *I have no teddy bear to hold,*
> *No room of my own, no place to go,*
> *Except my rock, my quiet place,*
> *To sit and watch the river flow*
> *My peaceful willows speak to me*
> *They whisper kind and loving words*
> *They hold no grudge, they do not judge*
> *Their branches sway with singing birds*
> *The finches and the starlings chirp*
> *The bobcats hunt along the path*
> *The frogs are croaking in the mud*
> *I cool my brow and calm my wrath*
> *My peaceful willows speak to me*
> *"Where are you going, where have you been?"*
> *I am a wandering, homeless soul*
> *My peaceful willows take me in*

228

Jolene *knew* he was *going* somewhere, despite all that "I am off for a walk" business.

So, Stevie, Jo and Tate trundled down the road with their gear, prepared to find Chuck's rock.

At the left side of the bridge, looking down into the river, Stevie said, "This can't be too hard—only a few dry rocks that could be the actual one."

"The rock's flat, don't you think? And in a place where he could be under the bridge but have a view of the opposite bank," suggested Tate, putting gloves on her guitarist's hands.

"That, and maybe something behind him to lean on. I can't imagine Chuck sitting straight up on a rock or with his back to the wildlife." This was Stevie, eyeing Jolene, who had not spoken during the walk.

Jolene took the notebook out of her backpack and read the poem aloud again. After a pause, she said, "He sat with his back to the concrete pillars."

She handed Stevie the notebook and began walking down the short path.

"Be careful down there," cautioned Stevie, "use your stick." She and Tate stashed their belongings under a bush and scrambled down the rocky, tangled path behind their English cousin, who was making for the thick concrete pillars that supported the Schulte Road Bridge.

Whacking their sticks before them (lions, tigers and bears aside, there *were* critters in the brush) the girls made their way to the edge of the bank under the bridge. The open metal grid was directly above them.

Jolene stood with her back to her cousins, looking intently at a big boulder, up against the side of the pillar facing north. She edged her way under the bridge, staying away from the slippery bank.

"He must have come down from the other side of the bridge," Tate whispered to Stevie.

"I think so, too, but let her go. We'll just follow."

The girls agreed.

In a moment, Jo was standing on the flat rock, looking across the river at the little animal path and a stand of swaying willow trees. The three girls sat down on the rock. Soon Tate climbed up the trail to retrieve their packs and get the red wagon as close as possible.

"This is it. I know it," said Jolene, with a little chill running through her as she realized she'd been here before, with Stevie and Tate five years ago.

At dusk, the job was done. They packed up and walked the quarter mile home.

Jock & Charlotte Take a Tour

et the children create their little ceremony, thought Charlotte. *Put Chuck to rest. It won't hurt anything.*

The dead... well, as Charlotte said, they don't give a fig what we do.

"Bad blood or not, it was stupid," said Jock, as he walked with Charlotte on the path over to Sweet Tea for their late breakfast on Tuesday morning. Jock's rolled up pant cuffs collected dust. His suspenders patterned with red and black ladybugs attracted hummingbirds.

Charlotte, cane in hand, was regal in her forest green hat, dark green suit, beige floppy-tied blouse and daytime pearls. And with Nana's lace-up, sturdy brown farm boots with thick wool socks (over the stockings), she was the true Lady Charlotte Huffington at Balmoral for a weekend Hunt. Sans foxes. Except Fox Wyman.

She said, "What was?"

"Chuck. Charles. What he did. Driving like that."

"Ah. 'A man might want to be stupid if it lets him do a thing his brain will not.' Or something like that."

Jock stopped in his tracks! "Close enough! *East of Eden!* Charlotte! I didn't know you read Steinbeck!"

"Oh, yes. Quite fond of American writers." *My, it will be even worse now,* she thought, *with endless time on my hands,* suddenly not looking forward to going home. *No wayward men to corral or worry over. No granddaughter nearby, perhaps. Books and tea, books and tea, endless cups of tea.*

"We're close by Mr. Steinbeck's haunts, are we not?"

"Yes! Yes! Would you like to see several places? I'd right like to take you! My family is bored senseless with Steinbeck by now."

And so, after breakfast, Jock and Charlotte went on a tour. Maria was happy enough for that! *Pour l'amour de Dieu! For the love of God, keep that woman busy, by all means!* Nana, too, was happy for the respite.

First, Point Lobos: they took the short drive down the coast to Whaler's Cove and walked down a trail to the beach where the seals lay gaily honking and rolling in the sand or sprawled across the boulders. The sea otters bobbed in the sunlit water, cracking abalone and clam shells with small rocks, twitching their whiskers and waving like saucy clowns.

"It wasn't planned, you know," said Charlotte.

Jock drove along Cannery Row—he pointed out the old canneries nested close to the wharves, where the early fishermen brought their catches of sardines, squid and abalone. He showed Charlotte Doc Ricketts' Lab and the shack where Steinbeck's Mack and the boys lived, dubbed the Palace Flophouse and Grill.

"Hmm," said Jock. Bravely, gently, he added, "Perhaps, like my dad used to say, 'accidentally on purpose'?"

They drove by the Great Tide Pool at Oceanview Avenue, where Doc Ricketts collected his specimens.

Jock treated Charlotte to her first cioppino at Fisherman's Grotto on the Wharf, where they sprinkled oyster crackers into the thick fishy soup and watched sailboats dip and sway in the Monterey Harbor.

"I'm not sure, Jock. I'll never be sure."

And then, a drive through the Corral de Tierra valley, the "fence of the earth," where the natural landscape confined the farm animals on the original Rancho Corral de Tierra.

"I'll never be sure about anything again," she said.

As they were driving east on Carmel Valley Road toward Sweet Farm, Charlotte asked Jock about the famous "pool" in the Carmel River, where Mack and the boys went on their frog hunting expedition in *Cannery Row*: "To sell their frogs to Doc Ricketts for a nickel a piece!" Charlotte exclaimed. "I remember!"

Jock turned onto Schulte Road, passed the Sweet Farm driveway and drove Charlotte to the Schulte Road Bridge—*So close to home!* she thought.

He parked the Cadillac at the right side of the bridge and helped Charlotte out, covering her shoulders with the car blanket to protect her from the late afternoon chill. They crossed the road to the left of the bridge and wandered a bit down the steep path.

Jock spoke about frogs:

"...here they'd be."

They stood quietly on the dirt trail, the Schulte Road Bridge to their right, the river shallow and dry in places, big rocks and boulders scattered among the brush and high grasses swishing under the one-lane bridge. Lady Charlotte leaned on her cane, listening to the wind whisper through the willow trees. She shivered and pulled the blanket tighter around her shoulders.

She thought of Charles as a boy, sitting on the stone bench in the formal gardens at her father the MP's home in the country. Little Charles wore grey shorts and a blue cashmere sweater over a white shirt. His mop of curly blonde hair was in his eyes, as always. And as always, Charles was alone.

Jock pointed east up river and said quietly, "The pool's about a quarter mile that way, Charlotte."

Something rooted them there: a silence of rustling leaves, a calm of afternoon light, a peace of place. A little red finch settled on a branch and whistled.

The Gathering

On Wednesday the sky was cloudless and at 8am, 60°—a perfect Carmel Valley morning. Saddle Mountain winked in the sunlight, and the Monterey Pines marching across the top of the hill were deep, dark green against the pale blue sky.

Nana awoke thinking about the young cousins planning Charles's Funeral at Sweet Farm, a "Gathering" they called it. It was just family—Chuck really didn't know anyone here, and she wasn't up to it, anyway. Charlotte had her own British arrangements to ponder, something both Nana and Jolene would be expected to attend in London after Thanksgiving, which meant being in England for the holidays.

At least we have some breathing room here, she sighed. A month.

And this Gathering gave Jolene something to do. In a creative way. Fox could keep the farm and harvest moving along, the girls can handle the Gathering.

Nana stretched in Jolene's bed, gazing at the ferns rustling at the window, and listened to Charlotte in Nana's own room across the hall, pulling herself together for this day.

For close to a week, this was the ritual: get up at 7, make coffee for herself and tea for Lady Charlotte, who waited, propped in her (Nana's) four poster bed, in a lacy pale blue bed-jacket, reading, with Nana's childhood "Quilt of White Roses" covering those substantial and very long legs.

Nana would give her the tea on a breakfast tray and go back to Jolene's bed, drink her coffee and listen for Lady Charlotte's discrete cough, which was Nana's signal to return to zip the Lady's corset. She then took Charlotte, usually with a full entourage in Poppy's car, to lunch or tea (except yesterday, thank you, Poppy).

She avoided talking about Charles, their relationship, money, debt, Jolene, the color of socks, or anything the least bit significant or provocative, have a drink punctually at 5pm in the Middle with Poppy and Mama and anyone else available, usually everyone, the more the better, dinner at 6:30, unzip the corset at 8.

And the rest of the day is mine.

 Stevie

We cousins huddled in the Hobbit waiting: as soon as the adults got their heads in the same place about the Gathering, which took forever according to our thinking, *we* made it happen.

We set up the borrowed Sweet Tea Room chairs on the grass in the shade of the oak tree that supported the Hobbit House on its sturdy little branches. 20 seats, including the two folders from the office, in a half circle.

Our big Poster on an easel propped by the tree described the program:

10am

Gather Together

by the Little Oak Tree

I'll Be Seeing You – Tate, guitar

A Few Words – Stevie

The Poem – My Peaceful Willows – Jo

The Flask – Stevie

The Tree – Stevie & Fáno

Starry Skies and Music – Everyone

Moon River – Tate

The Song – My Little Chickadee – Jo

Fly Me To the Moon – Tate, guitar

Brunch in the Sweet Tea Room

(Please bring your chair)

We spread a big flowered tablecloth over the red wagon to create an altar, draped Chuck's favorite blue tie around the neck of the urn that held half of his ashes, propped a framed, color-tinted black and white photo of Charles in his British Royal Navy uniform—an old one, but the classiest picture we had. We placed two black and white snapshots: Chuck at the piano, with cigarette and drink, and Chuck with Nana and Jo, in marginally happier days, circa 1957, sitting at their kitchen table in London. He was actually smiling. With a cigarette and a drink. Right.

Mama Maria provided a spray of lavender, rusty red fall mums and herbs in a tall vase, which we put behind the wagon/altar. In front was a small dried lavender wreath from Lavandula.

All Present: Nana, Jo, Tate, Stevie, Rita, Fox, Fáno, Jock, Maria, Charlotte, Farley Simpson and his parents, the Rodriguez family, the Johnsons, and Besty and Ace, Nana's friends.

We asked everyone to please not wear black but to come dressed for outside on Sweet Farm, which was a half-step up from *come as you are*: jeans and boots, best shirts and blouses, good sun hats.

And Lady Charlotte? Grey suit, pink blouse, black hat, with veil, etc. Short pearls, for two reasons: one, it was daytime and two, Charles's father had given her the pearls. She wore Nana's boots.

To my delight, she had tucked my dove feather gift into the band of her hat. (Even though technically she wasn't *my* grandmother, I was Carmel-izing her!)

Tate sat on a stool: her guitar rendition of "I'll Be Seeing You" made my lips tremble. I looked away from the seated guests to gather myself back into the bundle that was the 12-year-old me embodying my idea of a good reverend leading her flock, and turned to face them.

"We all know why we are here. To say goodbye to a member of our family, who has gone away.

Charles Wayland Huffington. I've never known anyone who died before. I am sorry to know someone now, and sorry it has to be Chuck or anyone I love. Jolene and Tate and I have talked a lot about Uncle Chuck the last few days, trying to imagine him, wherever he has gone. But there are so many possible and imaginative descriptions of that place, our minds got boggled and we had to stop. So, we talked about Chuck, the living Chuck. We don't know about that other place for sure, but we can tell you facts about the many faces of Chuck.

"We all have regrets. I have two: the peach I lifted from Felipe's Fruit Stand when I was seven; and something I said the other day about death that I would like to take back. But, assuming everybody takes regrets to the grave, then I say let the dead pack them away in dirt, and let's remember the great and distinguished and good things. Forever.

"So we made a list of all the Coolness of Uncle Chuck. First, he could play piano by ear. Anything. And if he didn't know it, he'd say, "Hummit," and he'd pick up the chords and melody right away. His songs were fun and goofy, and when he was in a good mood, he'd play them to make us laugh. He wrote songs for people on the spot, out of initials, or from words off a Post Toasties box.

"Chuck was a star rugby player, and an Eagle Scout. He held the door for women and would lay his coat down over a puddle for his mother, if necessary. He was a 10 year old pyromaniac and almost burned down their apartment once when his combustible chemistry set came in contact with the kitchen curtains. So he was curious.

"Aunt Nana told me they met when he asked to her to dance at a USO Club in London when she was there volunteering after the war and he "swept her off her feet." So, he could dance, too.

"Uncle Chuck encouraged Tate to play the guitar and sing her songs. He said she was a 'natural.' He said Stevie will be 'a famous author,' and he told Jolene, just the other day, to, uhm..." I faltered here, because Jolene was staring at me intently to keep from crying. My voice cracked when I said, "Chuck said, 'Joey, honey, be a star.'"

I waited a few seconds to let the frog jump out of my throat. Hghmph.

"Uncle Chuck was a poet. He never told anyone this: we came across this bit by accident when we went searching for music—in a notebook hidden in the piano bench." Nana raised an eyebrow at Jolene, who looked away.

"When we found his notebook, we read the poems, which were different from his song lyrics. Jo will read the one called "My Peaceful Willows." When we read this poem the other night, we knew what we would do to honor Chuck."

 # Jolene

I stood up on wobbly legs.

This rock is where I find my peace
The bridge protects me from all eyes
The willows are my tender friends
The moon shines in the starry skies
I have no teddy bear to hold,
No room of my own, no place to go,
Except my rock, my quiet place,
To sit and watch the river flow
My peaceful willows speak to me
They whisper kind and loving words
They hold no grudge, they do not judge
Their branches sway with singing birds
The finches and the starlings chirp
The bobcats hunt along the path
The frogs are croaking in the mud
I cool my brow and calm my wrath
My peaceful willows speak to me
Where are you going, where have you been?
I am a wandering, homeless soul
My peaceful willows take me in

"My Father was the only person who ever called me Joey. He was the first to give me a hankie for tears, after my budgie, Herbie died when I was six; he taught me how to ride a bike.

"My father was perplexed by life. I can't explain what happened, but I think some things are just inexplicable. One thing that is inexplicable is that I didn't really know my dad until he died. And now all I have is this notebook.

"After we found the book and read this poem, we walked to the Schulte Road Bridge." I pointed to the small hole dug by Fáno that morning.

 Stevie

We found his rock. It was too big to bring home in the little red wagon, so we brought small stones from nearby," I held up a basket.

"We retrieved this flask with his initials, CWH."

I stopped talking long enough to place the flask in the wagon. The light breeze whispered through the branches of the little oak.

"We brought home a tree to plant on Chuck's grave, so he will always have a friend, a Peaceful Willow," I indicated the small willow with roots wrapped in paper bags.

"We are going to take a moment to place Uncle Chuck's urn with his ashes into the grave with the flask and the wreath made of lavender stems." I moved to the grave with Fáno.

242

"In the Jewish tradition, people sit quietly with their loved ones for seven days to mourn the departed. Even though we are not Jewish, we think this is a good thing to do. If you look under your seat, you'll find a small paper bag of stars and moons and musical notes that Tate and I cut out for Chuck while the family was thinking about him dur-
ing the last week. There is also one of Chuck's handkerchiefs in each bag. Use it if you need to, keep it in his remembrance. He had 30 hankies with his initials."

Jolene stepped up once again, unplanned in our script, and said, "My dad may have been crazy and hard to deal with, he was always potted and did stupid things and got into trouble and spent money he didn't have and took blind risks which finally took his life, but he was a poet and a musician, a man with a heart, with a mind mixed up and twisted. He was ON-OFF, ON-OFF, like he was two distinct people inside, I don't know if the crazy one won." She looked around the circle. "That's all."

After Jolene stepped aside, I said, "When we have placed these things in the grave with Chuck, we would like everyone to take these stars and moons and musical notes in their hands and sprinkle them over Chuck's urn and the other things, so he will have stars, moonlight, music, friends and a good mar-tini wherever he is."

While Jo and Fáno and I quietly went about the business of burying Chuck, Tate played "Moon River" on her guitar.

My parents were the first to take the stars and notes in their hands and sprinkle. Everyone else followed, except Charlotte, Maria, and Jock, whose fingers were locked together. They were crying.

When all other stars and musical notes had been sprinkled, Charlotte and Maria got up with their bags of stars and moons and

notes in their hands and approached the grave together. Poppy followed.

Fáno finished planting the willow tree over Chuck (half of Chuck—can I stop saying that now?), surrounding it with the rocks from the river, while Tate played on, doodling chords and humming.

Rita gathered our people around the grave in a circle and instructed all to hold hands, and then Jo began to speak.

"One day last summer, before we came to Sweet Farm, my dad and I were in our living room in London. He had a cigarette and a drink." She smiled, "Well, duh."

We smiled with her.

"He was sitting at the piano. I had bubble gum, which I was blowing and popping. He was in a good mood. He wrote me this song, and this is how I would like to remember my dad, Charles Wayland Huffington:

"Come, my little Chickadee
Come sing this little ditty with me
Hum me a tune and I'll play along
Whistle me a lovely song

Give me some time and I'll write you a tune
And I'll be back for you in June
We'll set to sea and sale the ocean
Full of dreams and constant motion

Remember this when you are blue
That once I wrote a song for you
Sing to yourself or sing aloud
Sing to your friends or sing to a crowd

Remember the songs we played together
On sunny days and stormy weather
I'll play for you another day
I'll play to keep the blues away

Paint your skies and color your dreams
Follow the river where it streams
Do what you were meant to do
And I will write a song for you

Remember this when you are blue
That once I wrote a song for you."

The circle formed a human wreath, linked arms, swayed slightly, like lavender in the breeze. Maria and Charlotte held hands. Tate played *Fly Me to the Moon*, humming, holding us together for those precious last moments over Chuck's Carmel Valley resting place.

We broke up the circle slowly, knowing that when we did, Chuck would be in the past. I saw Charlotte and Maria in an embrace. "Look, Wena," my father whispered in my ear. "Out of bad, something good."

Rita and Juana went ahead to uncover the brunch: five quiche Lorraines, one quiche with broccoli, warm German potato salad, green salad, muffins, Charles's favorite toads in holes (popovers with hunks of sausage baked inside), coffee and tea.

We came in the door of the Sweet Tea Room, closed for the week due to "Family Matters," in ones and twos, quietly, murmuring, pensive. At the corner table, Jo shared the notebook with her mother, whose eyes welled with ancient tears. Lady Charlotte and Maria sat down together, laughing at the toads in holes, which reminded Charlotte of something Charles did as a child, which made Maria think of the time Nana put dandelions in the pancake batter. They would be sitting like this two hours later, having reminisced themselves right into nap time.

Jolene came and sat down with Tate and me at my favorite table, the one with the view of the prep area *and* the window. We were eating muffins with clotted cream, British-style, in her honor.

Jolene said, "My mother just told me Grand Mama Charlotte wants me to return to London with her. Like for good and all."

Chapter Four
The End

Stevie

No-o-o-o-o....

A bomb was dropped on our otherwise perfect day. And we were feeling so good about our send-off for Charles.

Now, I felt like I was going to throw up.

"No way. Are you going?" I whined like a petulant four-year-old.

"I... I don't know," said Jolene. "I can't put it all together in my head. I'll have to talk to her about it."

And she walked away, mystified—her thoughts speeding like a locomotive.

 Jolene

Later that day, Grand Mama Charlotte and I sat close to-gether on a bench in the garden by the Sweet Tea Room.

I was torn. I did love London. And I did want to go to Woolsley. And I did want to board, and be with my old friends, and pop down to Fortnum & Mason for tea on a Saturday with Grand Mama, retrieve my furniture and stuff and have everything be normal.

But nothing was normal, and I was exploring yet more new territory. My mother was a widow and I a half orphan and maybe a murderess. If I went to London, my father would not be there, any more than he was here.

But "here" was becoming "home," too, and there were Stevie and Tate, and the Hobbit House walls to paint.

Nana didn't know what she wanted, but she said she wouldn't stop me from going, if it was what I wanted.

I didn't know what I wanted.

I wanted my father back, is what I wanted.

At Stevie's suggestion, I told Fáno my "hanging upside down" dream.

As I began he stopped me and said, "Waz your father a student of the Tarot?"

I said, "What?"

And Fáno said, "Never mind. Go on, ma chérie."

Stevie, Fáno and I were sitting at the counter in the Chapel House kitchen.

I continued, "Like I said, he's hanging there, upside down. His knee is bent—the left one, I think. His hair is all, I don't know, glowing blonde, and long, and hanging down from his head, 'cause he's upside down, right? He's smiling, though, I remember that. It seems weird that he's upside-down and smiling. Then, all of a sudden, he's resting on the ground, on a blanket, with a basket and a picnic and there are people about: you, Stevie, everybody here. He's all happy and grinning, like the cat—the Cheshire Cat. He's wearing that yellow cashmere sweater I like, which I took out of his closet right after he died. It's under my pillow.

"That's it, then. I woke up—it was just before dawn, and that little bird, you know the one, Stevie, the little red finch that comes to my window in the Adobe? Well, he was outside your window, right by my little bed, saying hello. I know it was the same one. He has a little dot of black over one eye."

Fáno was quiet for a minute, Stevie busied herself with her colored pencils.

After a long pause, Fáno said, "ma chérie, I weel tell you what I believe. I theenk when theez happens, a loved one eez sending you a message from ze other place. People from every walk of life tell of theez visits: Catholic, Protestant, Jewish, Pagan, it doesn't matter. We are all ze same. In church, in ze forest, we find God where we find ze love. Don't tell anyone," he whispered, with a little grin. "Eet eez a beeg secret." We all laughed.

"We feel, mmmmm, energies. You know, our connection to our people, our true family, moves along different lines than what we see with our eyez. Tarot eez a deck of cards for divination—to connect to ze divine—and like dreams, theez cards bring us messages from ze spirit that eez een us and connects us, one to ze other. Your father appears to you like ze Hanged Man. He sends you a message. I'll get ze cards. One moment."

He disappeared into his and Rita's bedroom.

 Stevie

could see Jo's mind going over this like a cat sniffing provocative scent.

Over the next hour, Fáno went through the Tarot cards with Jo, using his Rider-Waite deck, which he shuffled through to find the Hanged Man. He showed it to Jolene, who let out a little "EEP!" and dropped the card. I picked it up. The Hanged Man was almost exactly like her dream, except in her dream, the Hanged Man had Chuck's face.

"You see, ma chérie, he eez smiling, which means, everything eez good. He eez fine upside down, he eez not in pain. He tells you, 'Do not worry, leetle one, I am okie dokie." We laughed again.

"He eez upside down because on his spiritual journey, he has learned many zhings that have set him on his head. He sees that right side up, upside down? Eet eez all ze same. When he stands upright again, he sees his world anew. From his new perspective. The picnic eez a happy thing, and he eez content to be that smiling cat.

And then he said, "I tell you theez, Jolene, do not rush into a decision about going to London. You can always go tomorrow."

Fáno said that religions were just the Creator in different clothes, and that he preferred not to be labeled. If he had a religion, it was a combination of Jesus's Golden Rule, Mysticism, Folklore and Mother Nature. He thought if we put our feet in the dirt every day and just opened our ears, we would hear.

Later, in the living room, Charlotte and Nana spoke. "She had to make that decision herself, you know that, Charlotte. This is no time for pressure on Jolene."

""Well aware of it, Nana. She's been through enough. I simply don't want her to throw away an opportunity. She is half-English, after all."

"Yes, and she's half us, too, American. She's a mongrel, perhaps a *heathen*, Charlotte, just like me. I think Jolene has two very good options before her, since all of her grandparents are in moods to back her education. This is all good. But to decide not to decide? That was brilliant. Good for her."

Lady Charlotte stood by the Cadillac in the driveway, waiting. She listened to the wind rustle the trees, and noticed the new one, the Peaceful Willow, over by the Hobbit House, swaying in the breeze. She thought she heard whistling, but she must have been mistaken. There was no one there.

It was the first time she'd really been alone on the Sweet Farm compound, other than in Nana's bed. She smelled the lavender and sage and oregano, she looked south and thought about that place under the Schulte Road Bridge, about her boy: gone.

The girls walked her down to the bridge the day after the Gathering, and she shivered once again, when she remembered her moments there with Jock and the vision of Charles.

Now, Jo, Stevie and Tate came walking down the path from the Tea Room.

254

"For your trip, Grand Mama. We packed your lunch. It's got everything you love: some scones, toads in holes, cookies and a thermos of tea."

"No," she said, hugging them all at once. She gathered them around her. "You're everything I love." And she meant it.

And so, the illustrious Lady Charlotte flew home to London, leaving some new friends behind her, waving.

She'd like to see those girls again—in fact, all of them. All of those hicks and heathens at Sweet Farm.

 Jolene

I reluctantly gave up the notebook to my mother after a few days of incessant reading and using it for a pillow, wrapped in the yellow cashmere sweater.

"I'd like to read what my husband said, Jolene. I want to be with it, just like you do. I lost him, too."

"You didn't love him, Mama. So you didn't really lose him. I loved him."

"Hghmph. I did love him. Maybe not as much as I should have, but I did love him. And he gave me you, so I loved him for that. But, no, I did not love him like I could have. It was all so mixed up. And, you do see that the craziness and the booze really killed it, don't you? He didn't give me anything to love, after a while. It's like, he spent it."

I got all that, I did. But, the fact was that if he had wanted her to read his poems, well, I thought that he would have shared them with her by now.

But, he was dead, so I presumed he didn't care anymore. And maybe I had killed him, so what right did I have to keep his thoughts to myself?

I gave her the notebook. Maybe it would help her put him to rest. I was still working on it myself. I gave her the notebook, but I kept the sweater.

I knew all the poems by heart now, anyway.

Nana

Nana slipped into Jock's study by way of the bathroom, softly closed the doors, wrapped her blue chenille robe around her for comfort, sat down at the small table, and picked up the phone.

It was past midnight, but after 8 am in London, so this was the only time to catch up with her party. She dialed the number, and waited.

'Allo?

"Ah. It's me."

"Oh, hello, you. So glad to hear from you. How's it going there? Did you get settled? How's Jolene? And Chuck? Fill me in. I love you."

"Oh, dear. I don't know quite where to start."

"Well, then first tell me why you are whispering. Must be quite late there."

"Yes, yes, it's after midnight, and everyone is asleep. This is my only moment. Actually, the only time I've been alone in days, except when I sequester myself in my room, and there's no phone in there. I just couldn't call before this. And, I knew you'd be getting home last night, so I waited..."

She was silent for a moment.

"Waited for what, darling? Has something happened?"

"Uhm. Yes. Well. It's Chuck. He's..."

"Ah, what's he done now? You OK?"

"Yes, I'm fine, William. But, Chuck... is dead."

Another long pause. "Oh, my dear, I am so sorry. So very sorry. What happened? Oh my dear..."

Nana filled her friend and paramour in on the saga of Chuck and his final days. She left nothing out, since William knew her well by now: knew her strange madness would be crossed with a giant load of guilt and a certain elation in being free of the daily torment.

"I am in an awful place about this, William. I don't quite know what to do."

"Did you tell him? About us, I mean."

"No, no. Then all the drama would become about that, he could just deflect everything onto me. So, no. But, I feel horrible, about him, about Jolene. Neither of them knows, er, knew, about us. Jolene still has no idea I was planning to bring her here anyway, even before Chuck exploded. The bit of money I put away is still in Wells Fargo Bank, since I couldn't let on about my escape plan. It would have been so much easier in the middle of the night. But, William, in the end there, at the flat in London, he scared me, for himself, for Jolene, for our lives, not because he'd hurt us on purpose, I don't think he would, but by doing something stupid, or not thinking, or drunk at the wheel, you know?"

"Well, he did do something stupid and drunk at the wheel, after all, didn't he? It was just a matter of time, Sweetheart."

"I know, I know. But like this? Did it have to be like this?"

London

Nana and Charlotte sat in the parlor, drinking tea laced with brandy and nibbling trimmed watercress sandwiches left over from the morning's reception in Charles's honor.

"It was a lovely service, don't you think, dear Nana?" asked Lady Charlotte, fishing for compliments.

She was so proud of herself, not only for her restraint, but of her choice of music and speakers for the day: Charles's cousin, Wilky Smythe, that rascal who was in the Royal British Navy with Charles, was admonished to *keep the liquor and other escapades out of his eulogy, if at all possible, and by all means, say whatever good things you like about dear Charles.* And Harmony Brooks, who...

Well, let's don't go on. We've had enough funerals for one story. It was a good day, everyone said goodbye to Charles, Lady Charlotte was able to bury her son with good British pomp, and also to keep down the conversations about exactly how he died and the facts regarding his messy heritage, and now Charlotte and Nana were alone. Jolene was out with her Woolsley School friends.

"It was lovely, Charlotte, really lovely. I am glad it's over, though," Nana said, taking off her shoes. She put her feet up on the small tapestried stool and let her head rest on the back of the forest green wingback chair. The fire was crackling and a light snow fluttered at the windows. It was a week before Christmas and Nana, torn between her beloved London and being at home with her family, let her mind wander.

Where does this all go from here? was the operative subject of her thoughts.

Charlotte interrupted Nana's reverie, "Nana? I said, This is for you."

Nana looked up from her fire-gazing trance, surprised.

"For me? What is it, Charlotte?"

"Something addressed to you in Charles's handwriting. It was here when I returned from California. It came with a note to me that said I wasn't to give it to you until after he... was buried, whenever that might be, and that I was to put it in my safety box at the bank until that time. I was... I thought it best to wait until after all the, ah, hoopla, before giving it to you. I don't know if it was the right thing to do or not, but it was my feeling, and the whole thing is kind of spooky, if you ask me, so there it is."

Nana took the envelope, studied it, waiting for it to speak, and then opened it.

She unfolded a bit of bulky paper. A small key dropped into her hand.

There was no note.

— END OF BOOK ONE —

Drawings by the author:

Bird's Eye View of the Farm

Barn Front Elevation

Chapel House Front Elevation

Barn Interior

Chapel House Interior

Adobe House Front Elevation

Adobe House Interior

Sweet Farm Bird's Eye View

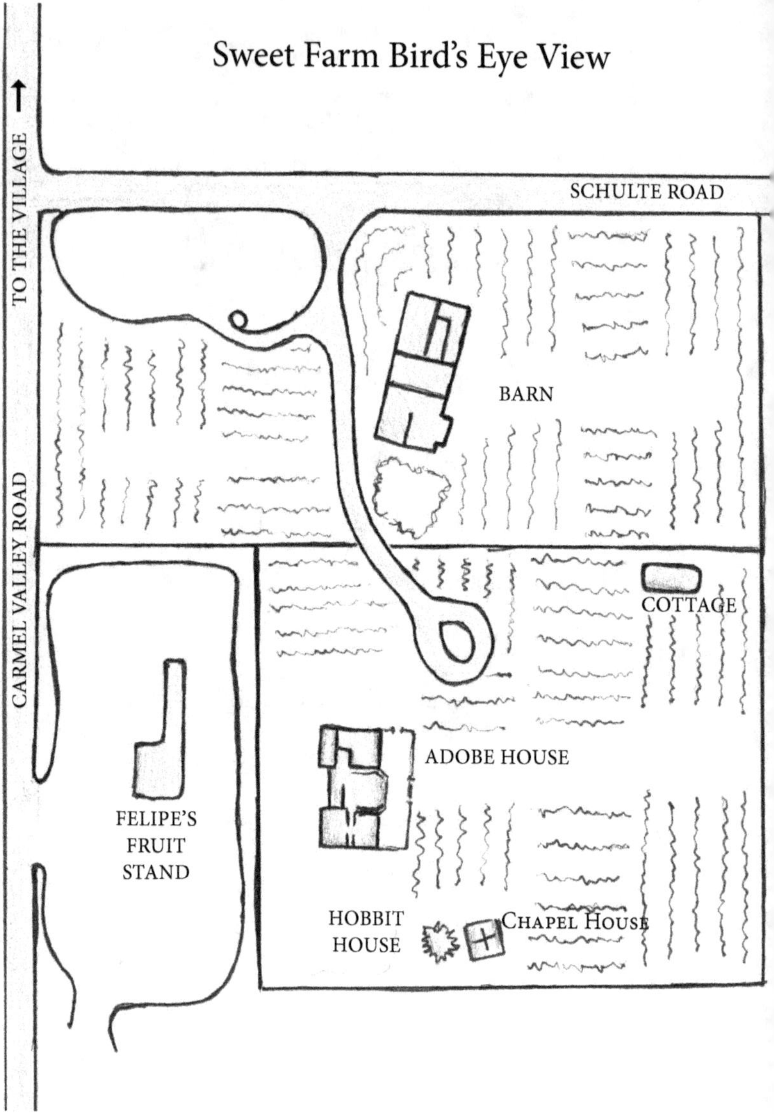

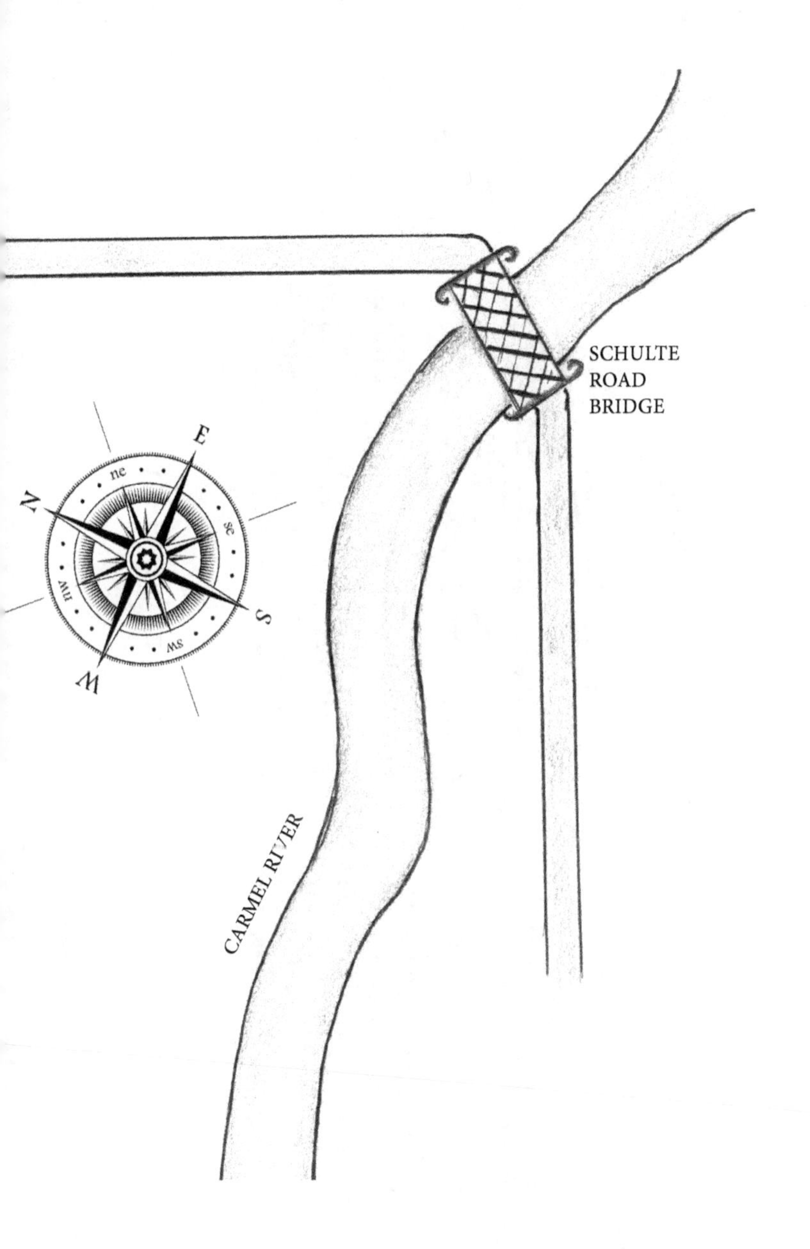

SCHULTE
ROAD
BRIDGE
E
ne
se
N
nw
S
W
sw
CARMEL RIVER

Barn Front Elevation

Chapel House
Front Elevation

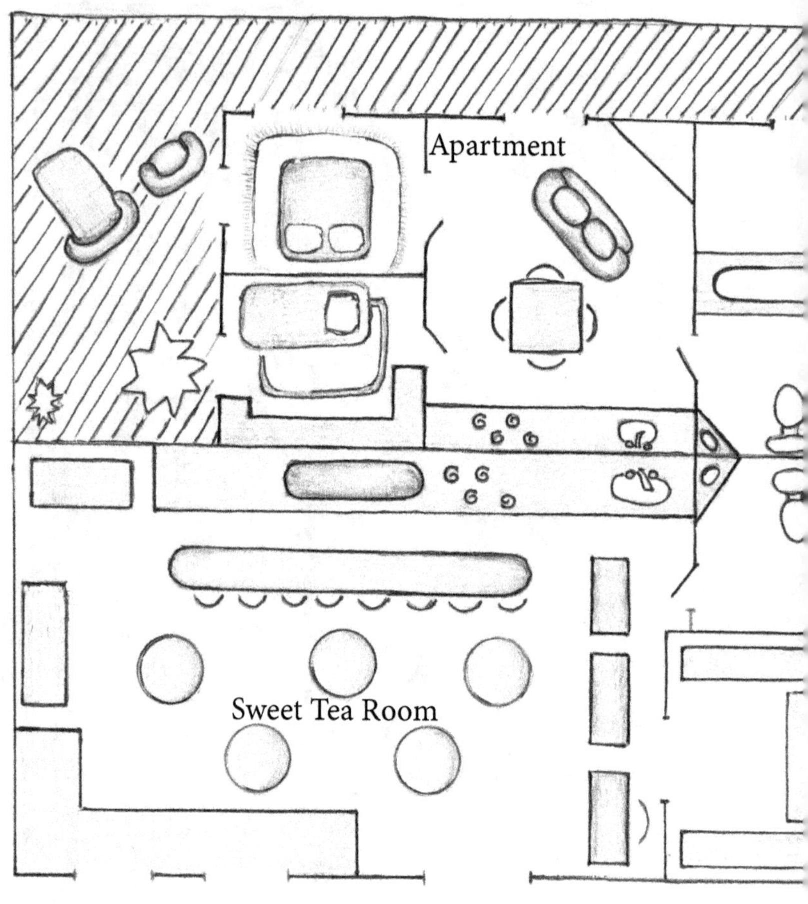

Barn Interior

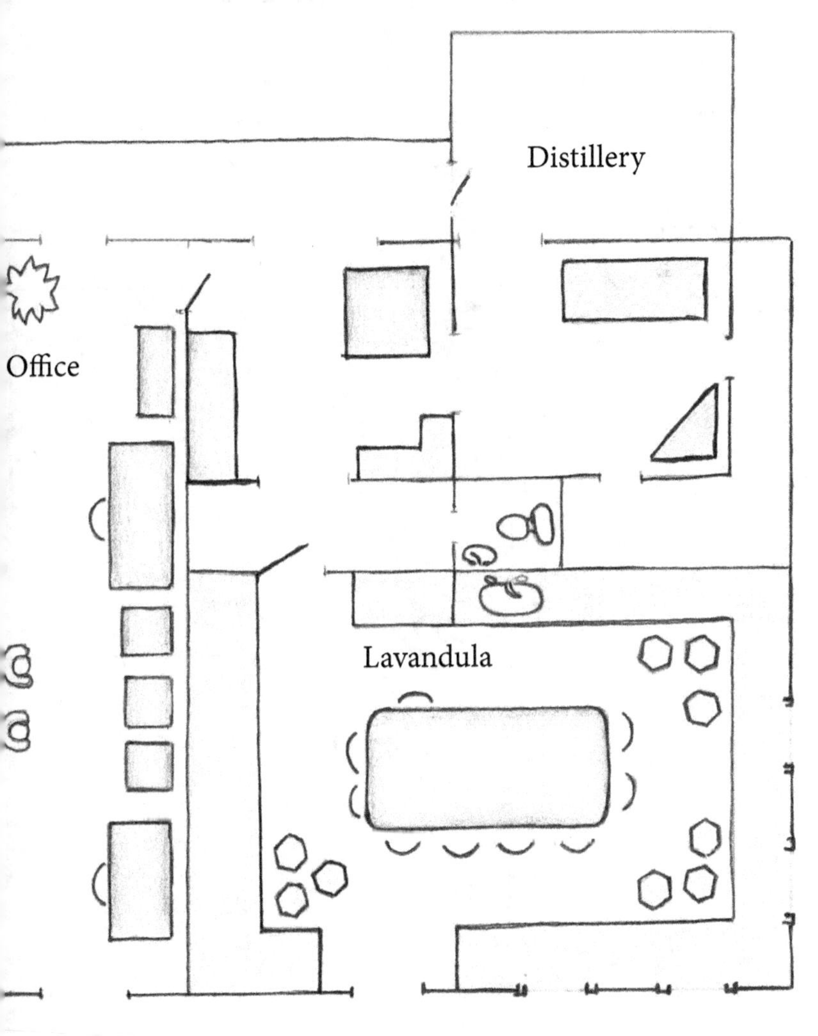

Distillery
Office
Lavandula

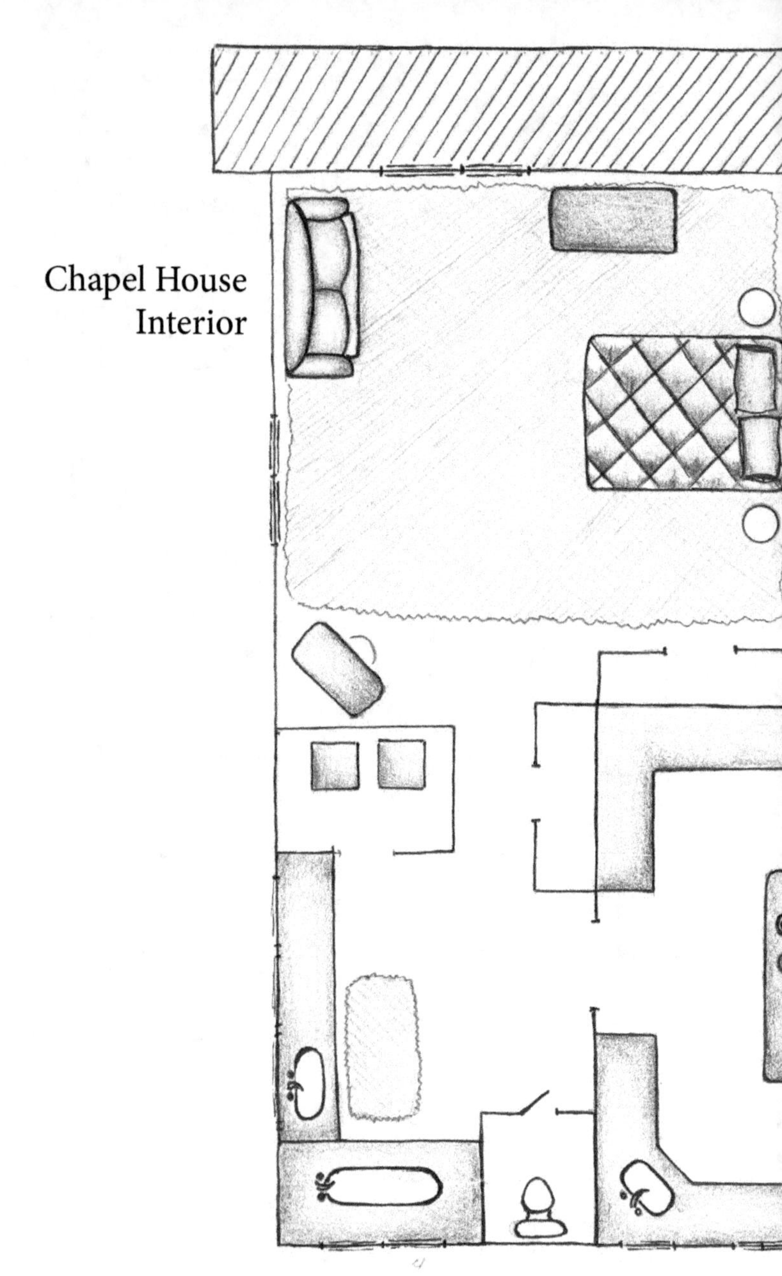

Chapel House
Interior

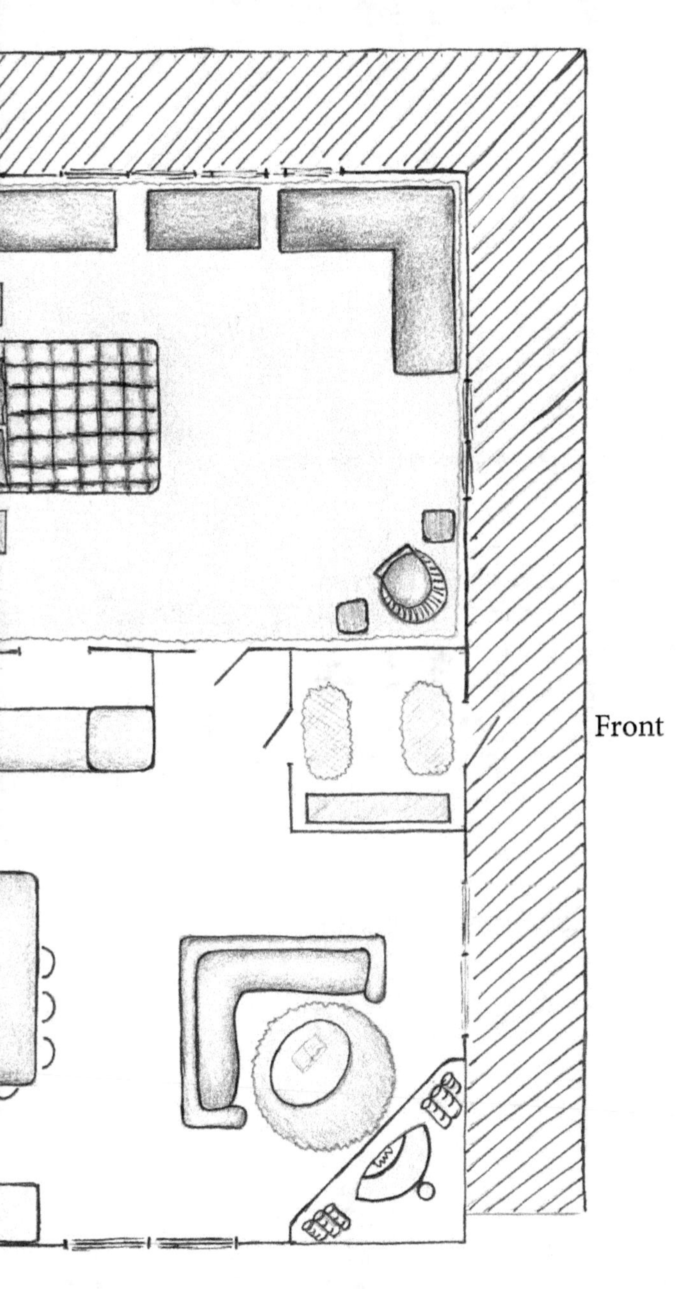

Front

Adobe House Front Elevation

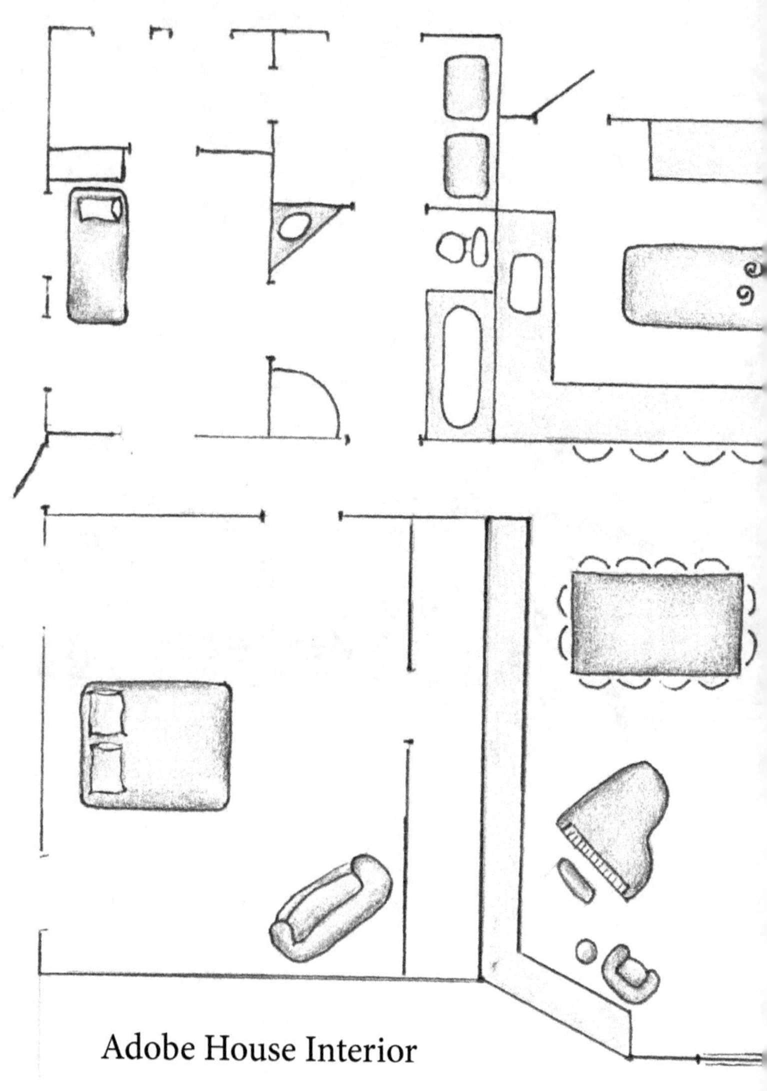

Adobe House Interior

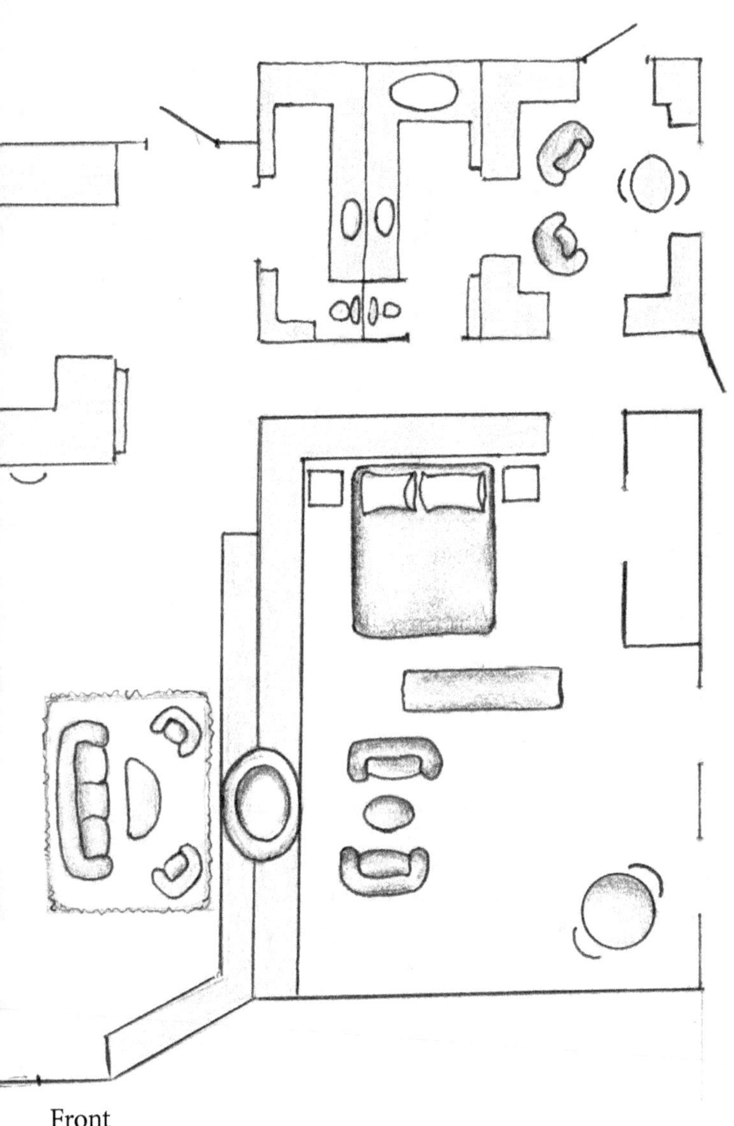

Front

Looking for John Steinbeck
Book One in *The Lavandula Series*
based on the fictional journals of Stefani Michel

Book designed and produced by Lucky Valley Press
Jacksonville, Oregon & Carmel, California
www.luckyvalleypress.com
Typeset in Minion, Kabel, and Bernhard Modern
All images in this book © 2016 by the artists

www.ingramcontent.com/pod-product-compliance
Lightning Source LLC
Chambersburg PA
CBHW072256130726
47910CB00012B/2024